THE RULING PASSION

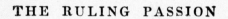

BY HENRY VAN DYKE

The Valley of Vision
Fighting for Peace
The Unknown Quantity
The Ruling Passion
The Blue Flower

———

Out-of-Doors in the Holy Land
Days Off
Little Rivers
Fisherman's Luck

———

Poems, Collection in one volume

———

Golden Stars
The Red Flower
The Grand Canyon, and Other Poems
The White Bees, and Other Poems
The Builders, and Other Poems
Music, and Other Poems
The Toiling of Felix, and Other Poems
The House of Rimmon

CHARLES SCRIBNER'S SONS

"I am the keeper of the light."

THE RULING PASSION

TALES OF NATURE AND
HUMAN NATURE

BY

HENRY VAN DYKE

WITH ILLUSTRATIONS
BY W. APPLETON CLARK

NEW YORK
CHARLES SCRIBNER'S SONS
MCMXIX

A WRITER'S REQUEST
OF HIS MASTER

LET me never tag a moral to a story, nor tell a story without a meaning. Make me respect my material so much that I dare not slight my work. Help me to deal very honestly with **words and with people** because they are both alive. Show me that as in a river, so in a writing, clearness is the best quality, and a little that is pure is worth more than much that is mixed. Teach me to see the local colour without being blind to the inner light. Give me an ideal that will stand the strain of weaving into human stuff on the loom of the real. Keep me from caring more for books than for folks, for art than for life. Steady me to do my full stint of work as well as I can: and when that is done, stop me, pay what wages Thou wilt, and help me to say,

from a quiet heart,

a grateful

AMEN.

PREFACE

In every life worth writing about there is a ruling passion,—"the very pulse of the machine." Unless you touch that, you are groping around outside of reality.

Sometimes it is romantic love: Nature's masterpiece of interested benevolence. In almost all lives this passion has its season of empire. Therefore, and rightly, it is the favourite theme of the storyteller. Romantic love interests almost everybody, because almost everybody knows something about it, or would like to know.

But there are other passions, no less real, which also have their place and power in human life. Some of them come earlier, and sometimes they last longer, than romantic love. They play alongside of it and are mixed up with it, now checking it, now advancing its flow and tingeing it with their own colour.

Just because love is so universal, it is often to one of the other passions that we must look for the distinctive hue, the individual quality of a life-story. Granted, if you will, that everybody must fall in love, or ought to fall in love, How will he do it? And what will he do afterwards? These are questions not without interest to one who watches the human drama as a friend. The answers depend upon those hidden and durable desires, affections, and impulses to which men and women give themselves up for rule and guidance.

Music, nature, children, honour, strife, revenge, money, pride, friendship, loyalty, duty,—to these objects and others like them the secret power of personal passion often turns, and the life unconsciously follows it, as the tides in the sea follow the moon in the sky.

When circumstances cross the ruling passion, when rocks lie in the way and winds are contrary, then things happen, characters emerge, slight events are significant, mere adventures are transformed into a real plot. What care I how many "hair-breadth 'scapes" and "moving accidents" your hero may pass through, unless I know him for a man? He is but a puppet strung on wires. His kisses are wooden and his wounds bleed sawdust. There is nothing about him to remember except his name, and perhaps a bit of dialect. Kill him or crown him,—what difference does it make?

But go the other way about your work:

> *"Take the least man of all mankind, as I;*
> *Look at his head and heart, find how and why*
> *He differs from his fellows utterly,"—*

and now there is something to tell, with a meaning.

If you tell it at length, it is a novel,—a painting. If you tell it in brief, it is a short story,—an etching. But the subject is always the same: the unseen, mysterious, ruling passion weaving the stuff of human nature into patterns wherein the soul is imaged and revealed.

PREFACE

To tell about some of these ruling passions, sim-ply, clearly, and concretely, is what I want to do in this book. The characters are chosen, for the most part, among plain people, because their feel-ings are expressed with fewer words and greater truth, not being costumed for social effect. The scene is laid on Nature's stage because I like to be out-of-doors, even when I am trying to think and learning to write.

"Avalon," Princeton, July 22, 1901.

CONTENTS

ILLUSTRATIONS

FROM DRAWINGS BY W. APPLETON CLARK

A LOVER OF MUSIC

A LOVER OF MUSIC

I

HE entered the backwoods village of Bytown literally on the wings of the wind. It whirled him along like a big snowflake, and dropped him at the door of Moody's "Sportsmen's Retreat," as if he were a New Year's gift from the North Pole. His coming seemed a mere chance; but perhaps there was something more in it, after all. At all events, you shall hear, if you will, the time and the manner of his arrival.

It was the last night of December, some thirty-five years ago. All the city sportsmen who had hunted the deer under Bill Moody's direction had long since retreated to their homes, leaving the little settlement on the border of the Adirondack wilderness wholly under the social direction of the natives.

The annual ball was in full swing in the dining-room of the hotel. At one side of the room the tables and chairs were piled up, with their legs projecting in the air like a thicket of very dead trees.

The huge stove in the southeast corner was blushing a rosy red through its thin coat of whitewash, and exhaling a furious dry heat flavoured with the smell of baked iron. At the north end, however, winter reigned; and there were tiny ridges of fine snow on the floor, sifted in by the wind through the cracks in the window-frames.

But the bouncing girls and the heavy-footed guides and lumbermen who filled the ball-room did not appear to mind the heat or the cold. They balanced and "sashayed" from the tropics to the arctic circle. They swung at corners and made "ladies' change" all through the temperate zone. They stamped their feet and did double-shuffles until the floor trembled beneath them. The tin lamp-reflectors on the walls rattled like castanets.

There was only one drawback to the hilarity of the occasion. The band, which was usually imported from Sandy River Forks for such festivities,—a fiddle, a cornet, a flute, and an accordion,—had not arrived. There was a general idea that the mail-sleigh, in which the musicians were to travel, had been delayed by the storm, and might break its way through the snow-drifts and arrive at any moment. But Bill Moody, who was naturally of a pessimistic temperament, had offered a different explanation.

"I tell ye, old Baker's got that blame' band down to his hotel at the Falls now, makin' 'em play fer his party. Them music fellers is onsartin; can't trust 'em to keep anythin' 'cept the toon, and they don't alluz keep that. Guess we might uz well shet up this ball, or go to work playin' games."

At this proposal a thick gloom had fallen over the assembly; but it had been dispersed by Serena Moody's cheerful offer to have the small melodion brought out of the parlour, and to play for dancing as well as she could. The company agreed that she was a smart girl, and prepared to accept her performance with enthusiasm. As the dance went on, there were frequent comments of approval to encourage her in the labour of love.

"Sereny's doin' splendid, ain't she?" said the other girls.

To which the men replied, "You bet! The playin''s reel nice, and good 'nough fer anybody—outside o' city folks."

But Serena's repertory was weak, though her spirit was willing. There was an unspoken sentiment among the men that "The Sweet By and By" was not quite the best tune in the world for a quadrille. A Sunday-school hymn, no matter how rapidly it was rendered, seemed to fall short of the necessary vivacity for a polka. Besides, the wheezy little organ positively refused to go faster than a certain gait. Hose Ransom expressed the popular opinion of the instrument, after a figure in which he and his partner had been half a bar ahead of the music from start to finish, when he said:

"By Jolly! that old maloney may be chock full o' relijun and po'try; but it ain't got no *dance* into it, no more 'n a saw-mill."

This was the situation of affairs inside of Moody's tavern on New Year's Eve. But outside of the house the snow lay two feet deep on the level, and shoulder-high in the drifts. The sky was at last swept clean of clouds. The shivering stars and the shrunken moon looked infinitely remote in the black vault of heaven. The frozen lake, on which the ice was three feet thick and solid as rock, was like a vast, smooth bed, covered with a white counterpane. The cruel wind still poured out of the northwest, driving the dry snow along with it like a mist of powdered diamonds.

Enveloped in this dazzling, pungent atmosphere, half blinded and bewildered by it, buffeted and yet supported by the onrushing torrent of air, a man on snow-shoes, with a light pack on his shoulders, emerged from the shelter of the Three Sisters' Islands, and staggered straight on, down the lake. He passed the headland of the bay where Moody's tavern is ensconced, and probably would have drifted on beyond it, to the marsh at the lower end of the lake, but for the yellow glare of the ball-room windows and the sound of music and dancing which came out to him suddenly through a lull in the wind.

He turned to the right, climbed over the low wall of broken ice-blocks that bordered the lake, and pushed up the gentle slope to the open passage-way by which the two parts of the rambling house were joined together. Crossing the porch with the last remnant of his strength, he lifted his hand to knock, and fell heavily against the side door.

The noise, heard through the confusion within, awakened curiosity and conjecture.

Just as when a letter comes to a forest cabin, it is turned over and over, and many guesses are made as to the handwriting and the authorship before it occurs to any one to open it and see who sent it, so was this rude knocking at the gate the occasion of argument among the rustic revellers as to what it might portend. Some thought it was the arrival of the belated band. Others supposed the sound betokened a descent of the Corey clan from the Upper Lake, or a change of heart on the part of old Dan Dunning, who had refused to attend the ball because they would not allow him to call out the figures. The guesses were various; but no one thought of the possible arrival of a stranger at such an hour on such a night, until Serena suggested that it would be a good plan to open the door. Then the unbidden guest was discovered lying benumbed along the threshold.

There was no want of knowledge as to what should be done with a half-frozen man, and no lack of ready hands to do it. They carried him not to the warm stove, but into the semi-arctic region of the parlour. They rubbed his face and his hands vigorously with snow. They gave him a drink of hot tea flavoured with whiskey—or perhaps it was a drink of whiskey with a little hot tea in it—and then, as his senses began to return to him, they rolled him in a blanket and left him on a sofa to thaw out gradually, while they went on with the dance.

Naturally, he was the favourite subject of conversation for the next hour.

"Who is he, anyhow? I never seen 'im before. Where'd he come from?" asked the girls.

"I dunno," said Bill Moody; "he did n't say much. Talk seemed all froze up. Frenchy, 'cordin' to what he did say. Guess he must a come from Canady, workin' on a lumber job up Raquette River way. Got bounced out o' the camp, p'raps. All them Frenchies is queer."

This summary of national character appeared to command general assent.

"Yaas," said Hose Ransom, "did ye take note

how he hung on to that pack o' his'n all the time?
Would n't let go on it. Wonder what 't wuz? Seemed
kinder holler 'n light, fer all 't wuz so big an' wropped
up in lots o' coverin's."

"What's the use of wonderin'?" said one of the
younger boys; "find out later on. Now's the time
fer dancin'. Whoop 'er up!"

So the sound of revelry swept on again in full
flood. The men and maids went careering up and
down the room. Serena's willing fingers laboured
patiently over the yellow keys of the reluctant melodion. But the ancient instrument was weakening
under the strain; the bellows creaked; the notes
grew more and more asthmatic.

"Hold the Fort" was the tune, "Money Musk"
was the dance; and it was a preposterously bad fit.
The figure was tangled up like a fishing-line after
trolling all day without a swivel. The dancers were
doing their best, determined to be happy, as cheerful as possible, but all out of time. The organ was
whirring and gasping and groaning for breath.

Suddenly a new music filled the room.

The right tune—the real old joyful "Money

Musk," played jubilantly, triumphantly, irresistibly
—on a fiddle!

The melodion gave one final gasp of surprise and
was dumb.

Every one looked up. There, in the parlour door,
stood the stranger, with his coat off, his violin
hugged close under his chin, his right arm making
the bow fly over the strings, his black eyes sparkling,
and his stockinged feet marking time to the tune.

"*Dansez! dansez*," he cried, "*en avant!* Don' spik'.
Don' res'! Ah 'll goin' play de feedle fo' yo' jess moch
yo' lak', eef yo' h'only *danse!*"

The music gushed from the bow like water from
the rock when Moses touched it. Tune followed tune
with endless fluency and variety—polkas, galops,
reels, jigs, quadrilles; fragments of airs from many
lands—"The Fisher's Hornpipe," "Charlie is my
Darling," "Marianne s'en va-t-au Moulin," "Petit
Jean," "Jordan is a Hard Road to Trabbel," woven
together after the strangest fashion and set to the
liveliest cadence.

It was a magical performance. No one could with-
stand it. They all danced together, like the leaves

11

on the shivering poplars when the wind blows through them. The gentle Serena was swept away from her stool at the organ as if she were a little canoe drawn into the rapids, and Bill Moody stepped high and cut pigeon-wings that had been forgotten for a generation. It was long after midnight when the dancers paused, breathless and exhausted.

"Waal," said Hose Ransom, "that's jess the high-tonedest music we ever had to Bytown. You're a reel player, Frenchy, that's what you are. What's your name? Where'd you come from? Where you goin' to? What brought you here, anyhow?"

"*Moi?*" said the fiddler, dropping his bow and taking a long breath. "Mah nem Jacques Tremblay. Ah'll ben come fraum Kebeck. W'ere goin'? Ah donno. Prob'ly Ah'll stop dis place, eef yo' lak' dat feedle so moch, hein?"

His hand passed caressingly over the smooth brown wood of the violin. He drew it up close to his face again, as if he would have kissed it, while his eyes wandered timidly around the circle of listeners, and rested at last, with a question in them, on

12

the face of the hotel-keeper. Moody was fairly warmed, for once, out of his customary temper of mistrust and indecision. He spoke up promptly.

"You kin stop here jess long's you like. We don' care where you come from, an' you need n't to go no fu'ther, 'less you wanter. But we ain't got no use for French names round here. Guess we'll call him Fiddlin' Jack, hey, Sereny? He kin do the chores in the day-time, an' play the fiddle at night."

This was the way in which Bytown came to have a lover of music among its permanent inhabitants.

II

JACQUES dropped into his place and filled it as if it had been made for him. There was something in his disposition that seemed to fit him for just the rôle that was vacant in the social drama of the settlement. It was not a serious, important, responsible part, like that of a farmer, or a store-keeper, or a professional hunter. It was rather an addition to the regular programme of existence, something unannounced and voluntary, and therefore not weighted with too heavy responsibilities. There was a touch of the transient and uncertain about it. He seemed like a perpetual visitor; and yet he stayed on as steadily as a native, never showing, from the first, the slightest wish or intention to leave the woodland village.

I do not mean that he was an idler. Bytown had not yet arrived at that stage of civilization in which an ornamental element is supported at the public expense.

He worked for his living, and earned it. He was full of a quick, cheerful industry; and there was nothing that needed to be done about Moody's establishment, from the wood-pile to the ice-house, at which he did not bear a hand willingly and well.

"He kin work like a beaver," said Bill Moody, talking the stranger over down at the post-office one day; "but I don't b'lieve he's got much ambition. Jess does his work and takes his wages, and then gits his fiddle out and plays."

"Tell ye what," said Hose Ransom, who set up for the village philosopher, "he ain't got no 'magination. That's what makes men slack. He don't know what it means to rise in the world; don't care fer

anythin' ez much ez he does fer his music. He's
jess like a bird; let him have 'nough to eat and a
chance to sing, and he's all right. What's he 'mag-
ine about a house of his own, and a barn, and sich
things?"

Hosea's illustration was suggested by his own experience. He had just put the profits of his last
summer's guiding into a new barn, and his imagination was already at work planning an addition to
his house in the shape of a kitchen L.

But in spite of his tone of contempt, he had a
kindly feeling for the unambitious fiddler. Indeed,
this was the attitude of pretty much every one in
the community. A few men of the rougher sort had
made fun of him at first, and there had been one or
two attempts at rude handling. But Jacques was determined to take no offence; and he was so good-
humoured, so obliging, so pleasant in his way of
whistling and singing about his work, that all un-
friendliness soon died out.

He had literally played his way into the affections
of the village. The winter seemed to pass more
swiftly and merrily than it had done before the vio-

lin was there. He was always ready to bring it out, and draw all kinds of music from its strings, as long as any one wanted to listen or to dance.

It made no difference whether there was a roomful of listeners, or only a couple. Fiddlin' Jack was just as glad to play. With a little, quiet audience, he loved to try the quaint, plaintive airs of the old French songs—"À la Claire Fontaine," "Un Canadien Errant," and "Isabeau s'y Promene"—and bits of simple melody from the great composers, and familiar Scotch and English ballads—things that he had picked up heaven knows where, and into which he put a world of meaning, sad and sweet.

He was at his best in this vein when he was alone with Serena in the kitchen—she with a piece of sewing in her lap, sitting beside the lamp; he in the corner by the stove, with the brown violin tucked under his chin, wandering on from one air to another, and perfectly content if she looked up now and then from her work and told him that she liked the tune.

Serena was a pretty girl, with smooth, silky hair, and eyes of the colour of the nodding harebells that

Perfectly content if she looked up now and then

blossom on the edge of the woods. She was slight and delicate. The neighbours called her sickly; and a great doctor from Philadelphia who had spent a summer at Bytown had put his ear to her chest, and looked grave, and said that she ought to winter in a mild climate. That was before people had discovered the Adirondacks as a sanitarium for consumptives.

But the inhabitants of Bytown were not in the way of paying much attention to the theories of physicians in regard to climate. They held that if you were rugged, it was a great advantage, almost a virtue; but if you were sickly, you just had to make the best of it, and get along with the weather as well as you could.

So Serena stayed at home and adapted herself very cheerfully to the situation. She kept indoors in winter more than the other girls, and had a quieter way about her; but you would never have called her an invalid. There was only a clearer blue in her eyes, and a smoother lustre on her brown hair, and a brighter spot of red on her cheek. She was particularly fond of reading and of music. It was this that made her so glad of the arrival of the violin. The violin's master knew it, and turned to her as a sympathetic soul. I think he liked her eyes too, and the soft tones of her voice. He was a sentimentalist, this little Canadian, for all he was so merry; and love—but that comes later.

"Where 'd you get your fiddle, Jack?" said Serena, one night as they sat together in the kitchen.

"Ah 'll get heem in Kebeck," answered Jacques, passing his hand lightly over the instrument, as he always did when any one spoke of it. "Vair' nice *violon*, hein? W'at you t'ink? Ma h'ole teacher, to de College, he was gif' me dat *violon*, w'en Ah was gone away to de woods."

"I want to know! Were you in the College? What 'd you go off to the woods for?"

"Ah 'll get tire' fraum dat teachin'—read, read, read, h'all taim'. Ah 'll not lak' dat so moch. Rader be out-door—run aroun'—paddle de *canot*—go wid de boys in de woods—mek' dem dance at ma *musique*. A-a-ah! Dat was fon! P'raps you t'ink dat not good, hein? You t'ink Jacques one beeg fool, Ah suppose?"

"I dunno," said Serena, declining to commit herself, but pressing on gently, as women do, to the

18

point she had in view when she began the talk.
"Dunno 's you 're any more foolish than a man that
keeps on doin' what he don't like. But what made
you come away from the boys in the woods and
travel down this way?"

A shade passed over the face of Jacques. He
turned away from the lamp and bent over the violin
on his knees, fingering the strings nervously. Then
he spoke, in a changed, shaken voice.

"Ah 'll tole you somet'ing, Ma'amselle Seréne. You
ma frien'. Don' you h'ask me dat reason of it no
more. Dat 's somet'ing vair' bad, bad, bad. Ah can't
nevair tole dat—nevair."

There was something in the way he said it that
gave a check to her gentle curiosity and turned it
into pity. A man with a secret in his life? It was a
new element in her experience; like a chapter in a
book. She was lady enough at heart to respect his
silence. She kept away from the forbidden ground.
But the knowledge that it was there gave a new
interest to Jacques and his music. She embroidered
some strange romances around that secret while she
sat in the kitchen sewing.

Other people at Bytown were less forbearing. They tried their best to find out something about Fiddlin' Jack's past, but he was not communicative. He talked about Canada. All Canadians do. But about himself? No.

If the questions became too pressing, he would try to play himself away from his inquisitors with new tunes. If that did not succeed, he would take the violin under his arm and slip quickly out of the room. And if you had followed him at such a time, you would have heard him drawing strange, melancholy music from the instrument, sitting alone in the barn, or in the darkness of his own room in the garret.

Once, and only once, he seemed to come near betraying himself. This was how it happened.

There was a party at Moody's one night, and Bull Corey had come down from the Upper Lake and filled himself up with whiskey.

Bull was an ugly-tempered fellow. The more he drank, up to a certain point, the steadier he got on his legs, and the more necessary it seemed for him to fight somebody. The tide of his pugnacity that night took a straight set toward Fiddlin' Jack.

Bull began with musical criticisms. The fiddling did not suit him at all. It was too quick, or else it was too slow. He failed to perceive how any one could tolerate such music even in the infernal regions, and he expressed himself in plain words to that effect. In fact, he damned the performance without even the faintest praise.

But the majority of the audience gave him no support. On the contrary, they told him to shut up. And Jack fiddled along cheerfully.

Then Bull returned to the attack, after having fortified himself in the bar-room. And now he took national grounds. The French were, in his opinion, a most despicable race. They were not a patch on the noble American race. They talked too much, and their language was ridiculous. They had a condemned, fool habit of taking off their hats when they spoke to a lady. They ate frogs.

Having delivered himself of these sentiments in a loud voice, much to the interruption of the music, he marched over to the table on which Fiddlin' Jack was sitting, and grabbed the violin from his hands.

"Gimme that dam' fiddle," he cried, "till I see if there's a frog in it."

Jacques leaped from the table, transported with rage. His face was convulsed. His eyes blazed. He snatched a carving-knife from the dresser behind him, and sprang at Corey.

"*Tort Dieu!*" he shrieked, "*mon violon!* Ah'll keel you, beast!"

But he could not reach the enemy. Bill Moody's long arms were flung around the struggling fiddler, and a pair of brawny guides had Corey pinned by the elbows, hustling him backward. Half a dozen men thrust themselves between the would-be combatants. There was a dead silence, a scuffling of feet on the bare floor; then the danger was past, and a tumult of talk burst forth.

But a strange alteration had passed over Jacques. He trembled. He turned white. Tears poured down his cheeks. As Moody let him go, he dropped on his knees, hid his face in his hands, and prayed in his own tongue.

"My God, it is here again! Was it not enough that I must be tempted once before? Must I have the madness yet another time? My God, show the mercy toward me, for the Blessed Virgin's sake. I am a sinner, but not the second time; for the love of Jesus, not the second time! *Ave Maria, gratia plena, ora pro me!*"

The others did not understand what he was saying. Indeed, they paid little attention to him. They saw he was frightened, and thought it was with fear. They were already discussing what ought to be done about the fracas.

It was plain that Bull Corey, whose liquor had now taken effect suddenly, and made him as limp as a strip of cedar bark, must be thrown out of the door, and left to cool off on the beach. But what to do with Fiddlin' Jack for his attempt at knifing—a detested crime? He might have gone at Bull with a gun, or with a club, or with a chair, or with any recognized weapon. But with a carving-knife! That was a serious offence. Arrest him, and send him to jail at the Forks? Take him out, and duck him in the lake? Lick him, and drive him out of the town?

There was a multitude of counsellors, but it was

Hose Ransom who settled the case. He was a well-known fighting-man, and a respected philosopher. He swung his broad frame in front of the fiddler.

"Tell ye what we'll do. Jess nothin'! Ain't Bull Corey the blowin'est and the mos' trouble-us cuss 'round these hull woods? And wouldn't it be a fust-rate thing ef some o' the wind was let out 'n him?"

General assent greeted this pointed inquiry.

"And wa'n't Fiddlin' Jack peacerble 'nough 's long 's he was let alone? What's the matter with lettin' him alone now?"

The argument seemed to carry weight. Hose saw his advantage, and clinched it.

"Ain't he given us a lot o' fun here this winter in a innercent kind o' way, with his old fiddle? I guess there ain't nothin' on airth he loves better 'n that holler piece o' wood, and the toons that's inside o' it. It's jess like a wife or a child to him. Where's that fiddle, anyhow?"

Some one had picked it deftly out of Corey's hand during the scuffle, and now passed it up to Hose.

"Here, Frenchy, take yer long-necked, pot-bellied

music-gourd. And I want you boys to understand, ef any one teches that fiddle ag'in, I'll knock hell out 'n him."

So the recording angel dropped another tear upo... the record of Hosea Ransom, and the books were closed for the night.

III

FOR some weeks after the incident of the violin and the carving-knife, it looked as if a permanent cloud had settled upon the spirits of Fiddlin' Jack. He was sad and nervous; if any one touched him, or even spoke to him suddenly, he would jump like a deer. He kept out of everybody's way as much as possible, sat out in the wood-shed when he was not at work, and could not be persuaded to bring down his fiddle. He seemed in a fair way to be transformed into "the melancholy Jaques."

It was Serena who broke the spell; and she did it in a woman's way, the simplest way in the world — by taking no notice of it.

"Ain't you goin' to play for me to-night?" she

asked one evening, as Jacques passed through the kitchen. Whereupon the evil spirit was exorcised, and the violin came back again to its place in the life of the house.

But there was less time for music now than there had been in the winter. As the snow vanished from the woods, and the frost leaked out of the ground, and the ice on the lake was honeycombed, breaking away from the shore, and finally going to pieces altogether in a warm southeast storm, the Sportsmen's Retreat began to prepare for business. There was a garden to be planted, and there were boats to be painted. The rotten old wharf in front of the house stood badly in need of repairs. The fiddler proved himself a Jack-of-all-trades and master of more than one.

In the middle of May the anglers began to arrive at the Retreat—a quiet, sociable, friendly set of men, most of whom were old-time acquaintances, and familiar lovers of the woods. They belonged to the "early Adirondack period," these disciples of Walton. They were not very rich, and they did not put on much style, but they understood how to have a good time; and what they did not know about fishing was not worth knowing.

Jacques fitted into their scheme of life as a well-made reel fits the butt of a good rod. He was a steady oarsman, a lucky fisherman, with a real genius for the use of the landing-net, and a cheerful companion, who did not insist upon giving his views about artificial flies and advice about casting, on every occasion. By the end of June he found himself in steady employment as a guide.

He liked best to go with the anglers who were not too energetic, but were satisfied to fish for a few hours in the morning and again at sunset, after a long rest in the middle of the afternoon. This was just the time for the violin; and if Jacques had his way, he would take it with him, carefully tucked away in its case in the bow of the boat; and when the pipes were lit after lunch, on the shore of Round Island or at the mouth of Cold Brook, he would discourse sweet music until the declining sun drew near the tree-tops and the veery rang his silver bell for vespers. Then it was time to fish again, and the flies danced merrily over the water, and the great speckled trout leaped eagerly to catch them. For trolling all day long for lake-trout Jacques had little liking.

"Dat is not de sport," he would say, "to hol' one r-r-ope in de 'and, an' den pool heem in wid one feesh on t'ree hook, h'all tangle h'up in hees mout' —dat is not de sport. Bisside, dat leef not taim' for *la musique.*"

Midsummer brought a new set of guests to the Retreat, and filled the ramshackle old house to over-flowing. The fishing fell off, but there were picnics and camping-parties in abundance, and Jacques was in demand. The ladies liked him; his manners were so pleasant, and they took a great interest in his music. Moody bought a piano for the parlour that summer; and there were two or three good players in the house, to whom Jacques would listen with delight, sitting on a pile of logs outside the parlour-windows in the warm August evenings.

Some one asked him whether he did not prefer the piano to the violin.

"*Non*," he answered, very decidedly; "dat piano, he vairee smart; he got plentee word, lak' de leetle yellow bird in de cage—'ow you call heem?—de

cánnarie. He spik' moch. Bot dat *violon*, he spik'
more deep, to de heart, lak' de *rossignol*. He mak'
me feel more glad, more sorree—dat fo' w'at Ah
lak' heem de bes'!"

Through all the occupations and pleasures of the
summer Jacques kept as near as he could to Serena.
If he learned a new tune, by listening to the piano
—some simple, artful air of Mozart, some melancholy echo of a nocturne of Chopin, some tender,
passionate love-song of Schubert—it was to her
that he would play it first. If he could persuade
her to a boat-ride with him on the lake, Sunday
evening, the week was complete. He even learned
to know the more shy and delicate forest-blossoms
that she preferred, and would come in from a day's
guiding with a tiny bunch of belated twin-flowers,
or a few purple-fringed orchids, or a handful of
nodding stalks of the fragrant pyrola, for her.

So the summer passed, and the autumn, with its
longer hunting expeditions into the depth of the
wilderness; and by the time winter came around
again, Fiddlin' Jack was well settled at Moody's as
a regular Adirondack guide of the old-fashioned

type, but with a difference. He improved in his English. Something of that missing quality which Moody called ambition, and to which Hose Ransom gave the name of imagination, seemed to awaken within him. He saved his wages. He went into business for himself in a modest way, and made a good turn in the manufacture of deerskin mittens and snow-shoes. By the spring he had nearly three hundred dollars laid by, and bought a piece of land from Ransom on the bank of the river just above the village.

The second summer of guiding brought him in enough to commence building a little house. It was of logs, neatly squared at the corners; and there was a door exactly in the middle of the façade, with a square window at either side, and another at each end of the house, according to the common style of architecture at Bytown.

But it was in the roof that the touch of distinction appeared. For this, Jacques had modelled after his memory of an old Canadian roof. There was a delicate concave sweep in it, as it sloped downward from the peak, and the eaves projected pleasantly over the front door, making a strip of shade wherein it would be good to rest when the afternoon sun shone hot.

He took great pride in this effort of the builder's art. One day at the beginning of May, when the house was nearly finished, he asked old Moody and Serena to stop on their way home from the village and see what he had done. He showed them the kitchen, and the living-room, with the bed-room partitioned off from it, and sharing half of its side window. Here was a place where a door could be cut at the back, and a shed built for a summer kitchen —for the coolness, you understand. And here were two stoves—one for the cooking, and the other in the living-room for the warming, both of the newest.

"An' look dat roof. Dat's lak' we make dem in Canada. De rain ron off easy, and de sun not shine too strong at de door. Ain't dat nice? You lak' dat roof, Ma'amselle Seréne, hein?"

Thus the imagination of Jacques unfolded itself, and his ambition appeared to be making plans for its accomplishment. I do not want any one to suppose that there was a crisis in his affair of the heart.

There was none. Indeed, it is very doubtful whether anybody in the village, even Serena herself, ever dreamed that there was such an affair. Up to the point when the house was finished and furnished, it was to be a secret between Jacques and his violin; and they found no difficulty in keeping it.

Bytown was a Yankee village. Jacques was, after all, nothing but a Frenchman. The native tone of religion, what there was of it, was strongly Methodist. Jacques never went to church, and if he was anything, was probably a Roman Catholic. Serena was something of a sentimentalist, and a great reader of novels; but the international love-story had not yet been invented, and the idea of getting married to a foreigner never entered her head. I do not say that she suspected nothing in the wild flowers, and the Sunday evening boat-rides, and the music. She was a woman. I have said already that she liked Jacques very much, and his violin pleased her to the heart. But the new building by the river? I am sure she never even thought of it once, in the way that he did.

Well, in the end of June, just after the furniture

had come for the house with the curved roof, Serena was married to Hose Ransom. He was a young
widower without children, and altogether the best
fellow, as well as the most prosperous, in the settlement. His house stood up on the hill, across the
road from the lot which Jacques had bought. It was
painted white, and it had a narrow front porch, with
a scroll-saw fringe around the edge of it; and there
was a little garden fenced in with white palings, in
which Sweet Williams and pansies and blue lupines
and pink bleeding-hearts were planted.

The wedding was at the Sportsmen's Retreat, and
Jacques was there, of course. There was nothing
of the disconsolate lover about him. The noun he
might have confessed to, in a confidential moment
of intercourse with his violin; but the adjective was
not in his line.

The strongest impulse in his nature was to be a
giver of entertainment, a source of joy in others, a
recognized element of delight in the little world
where he moved. He had the artistic temperament in
its most primitive and naïve form. Nothing pleased
him so much as the act of pleasing. Music was the

means which Nature had given him to fulfil this desire. He played, as you might say, out of a certain kind of selfishness, because he enjoyed making other people happy. He was selfish enough, in his way, to want the pleasure of making everybody feel the same delight that he felt in the clear tones, the merry cadences, the tender and caressing flow of his violin. That was consolation. That was power. That was success.

And especially was he selfish enough to want to feel his ability to give Serena a pleasure at her wedding—a pleasure that nobody else could give her. When she asked him to play, he consented gladly. Never had he drawn the bow across the strings with a more magical touch. The wedding guests danced as if they were enchanted. The big bridegroom came up and clapped him on the back, with the nearest approach to a gesture of affection that backwoods etiquette allows between men.

"Jack, you're the boss fiddler o' this hull county. Have a drink now? I guess you're mighty dry."

"*Merci, non,*" said Jacques. "I drink only de museek dis night. Eef I drink two t'ings, I get dronk."

In between the dances, and while the supper was going on, he played quieter tunes—ballads and songs that he knew Serena liked. After supper came the final reel; and when that was wound up, with immense hilarity, the company ran out to the side door of the tavern to shout a noisy farewell to the bridal buggy, as it drove down the road toward the house with the white palings. When they came back, the fiddler was gone. He had slipped away to the little cabin with the curved roof.

All night long he sat there playing in the dark. Every tune that he had ever known came back to him—grave and merry, light and sad. He played them over and over again, passing round and round among them as a leaf on a stream follows the eddies, now backward, now forward, and returning most frequently to an echo of a certain theme from Chopin—you remember the *nocturne in G minor*, the second one? He did not know who Chopin was. Perhaps he did not even know the name of the music. But the air had fallen upon his ear somewhere, and had stayed in his memory; and now it seemed to say something to him that had an especial meaning.

At last he let the bow fall. He patted the brown wood of the violin after his old fashion, loosened the strings a little, wrapped it in its green baize cover, and hung it on the wall.

"Hang thou there, thou little violin," he murmured. "It is now that I shall take the good care of thee, as never before; for thou art the wife of Jacques Tremblay. And the wife of 'Osée Ransom, she is a friend to us, both of us; and we will make the music for her many years, I tell thee, many years—for her, and for her good man, and for the children—yes?"

But Serena did not have many years to listen to the playing of Jacques Tremblay: on the white porch, in the summer evenings, with bleeding-hearts abloom in the garden; or by the winter fire, while the pale blue moonlight lay on the snow without, and the yellow lamplight filled the room with homely radiance. In the fourth year after her marriage she died, and Jacques stood beside Hose at the funeral.

There was a child—a little boy—delicate and blue-eyed, the living image of his mother. Jacques appointed himself general attendant, nurse in extraordinary, and court musician to this child. He gave up his work as a guide. It took him too much away from home. He was tired of it. Besides, what did he want of so much money? He had his house. He could gain enough for all his needs by making snow-shoes and the deerskin mittens at home. Then he could be near little Billy. It was pleasanter so.

When Hose was away on a long trip in the woods, Jacques would move up to the white house and stay on guard. His fiddle learned how to sing the prettiest slumber songs. Moreover, it could crow in the morning, just like the cock; and it could make a noise like a mouse, and like the cat, too; and there were more tunes inside of it than in any music-box in the world.

As the boy grew older, the little cabin with the curved roof became his favourite playground. It was near the river, and Fiddlin' Jack was always ready to make a boat for him, or help him catch minnows in the mill-dam. The child had a taste for music, too, and learned some of the old Canadian songs, which he sang in a curious broken *patois*, while his delighted teacher accompanied him on the violin.

37

But it was a great day when he was eight years old, and Jacques brought out a small fiddle, for which he had secretly sent to Albany, and presented it to the boy.

"You see dat feedle, Billee? Dat's for you! You mek' your lesson on dat. When you kin mek' de museek, den you play on de *violon*—lak' dis one— listen!"

Then he drew the bow across the strings and dashed into a medley of the jolliest airs imaginable.

The boy took to his instruction as kindly as could have been expected. School interrupted it a good deal; and play with the other boys carried him away often; but, after all, there was nothing that he liked much better than to sit in the little cabin on a winter evening and pick out a simple tune after his teacher. He must have had some talent for it, too; for Jacques was very proud of his pupil, and prophesied great things of him.

"You know dat little Billee of 'Ose Ransom," the fiddler would say to a circle of people at the hotel, where he still went to play for parties; "you know dat small Ransom boy? Well, I'm tichin' heem play

"Den you play on de *violon*—lak' dis one—listen!"

de feedle; an' I tell you, one day he play better dan hees ticher. Ah, dat's gr-r-reat t'ing, de museek, ain't it? Mek' you laugh, mek' you cry, mek' you dance! Now, you dance. Tek' your pardnerre. *En avant!* Kip' step to de museek!"

IV

THIRTY years brought many changes to Bytown. The wild woodland flavour evaporated out of the place almost entirely; and instead of an independent centre of rustic life, it became an annex to great cities. It was exploited as a summer resort, and discovered as a winter resort. Three or four big hotels were planted there, and in their shadow a score of boarding-houses alternately languished and flourished. The summer cottage also appeared and multiplied; and with it came many of the peculiar features which man elaborates in his struggle toward the finest civilization— afternoon teas, and amateur theatricals, and claw-hammer coats, and a casino, and even a few servants in livery.

The very name of Bytown was discarded as being

too American and commonplace. An Indian name was discovered, and considered much more romantic and appropriate. You will look in vain for Bytown on the map now. Nor will you find the old saw-mill there any longer, wasting a vast water-power to turn its dripping wheel and cut up a few pine-logs into fragrant boards. There is a big steam-mill a little farther up the river, which rips out thousands of feet of lumber in a day; but there are no more pine-logs, only sticks of spruce which the old lumbermen would have thought hardly worth cutting. And down below the dam there is a pulp-mill, to chew up the little trees and turn them into paper, and a chair factory, and two or three industrial establishments, with quite a little colony of French-Canadians employed in them as workmen.

Hose Ransom sold his place on the hill to one of the hotel companies, and a huge caravansary occupied the site of the house with the white palings. There were no more bleeding-hearts in the garden. There were beds of flaring red geraniums, which looked as if they were painted; and across the circle of smooth lawn in front of the piazza the name of the hotel was printed in alleged ornamental plants —letters two feet long, immensely ugly. Hose had been elevated to the office of postmaster, and lived in a Queen Antic cottage on the main street. Little Billy Ransom had grown up into a very interesting young man, with a decided musical genius, and a tenor voice, which being discovered by an enterprising patron of genius, from Boston, Billy was sent away to Paris to learn to sing. Some day you will hear of his début in grand opera, as *Monsieur Guillaume Rançon*.

But Fiddlin' Jack lived on in the little house with the curved roof, beside the river, refusing all the good offers which were made to him for his piece of land.

"*Non*," he said; "what for shall I sell dis house? I lak' her, she lak' me. All dese walls got full from museek, jus' lak' de wood of dis *violon*. He play bettair dan de new feedle, becos' I play heem so long. I lak' to lissen to dat rivaire in de night. She sing from long taim' ago—jus' de same song w'en I firs' come here. W'at for I go away? W'at I get? W'at you can gif' me lak' dat?"

He was still the favourite musician of the country-side, in great request at parties and weddings; but he had extended the sphere of his influence a little. He was not willing to go to church, though there were now several to choose from; but a young minister of liberal views who had come to take charge of the new Episcopal chapel had persuaded Jacques into the Sunday-school, to lead the children's singing with his violin. He did it so well that the school became the most popular in the village. It was much pleasanter to sing than to listen to long addresses.

Jacques grew old gracefully, but he certainly grew old rapidly. His beard was white; his shoulders were stooping; he suffered a good deal in damp days from rheumatism—fortunately not in his hands, but in his legs. One spring there was a long spell of abominable weather, just between freezing and thawing. He caught a heavy cold and took to his bed Hose came over to look after him.

For a few days the old fiddler kept up his courage, and would sit up in the bed trying to play; then his strength and his spirit seemed to fail together. He grew silent and indifferent. When Hose came in he would find Jacques with his face turned to the wall, where there was a tiny brass crucifix hanging below the violin, and his lips moving quietly.

"Don't ye want the fiddle, Jack? I'd like ter hear some o' them old-time tunes ag'in."

But the artifice failed. Jacques shook his head. His mind seemed to turn back to the time of his first arrival in the village, and beyond it. When he spoke at all, it was of something connected with this early time.

"Dat was bad taim' when I near keel Bull Corey, hein?"

Hose nodded gravely.

"Dat was beeg storm, dat night when I come to Bytown. You remember dat?"

Yes, Hose remembered it very well. It was a real old-fashioned storm.

"Ah, but befo' dose taim', dere was wuss taim' dan dat—in Canada. Nobody don' know 'bout dat. I lak' to tell you, 'Ose, but I can't. No, it is not possible to tell dat, nevair!"

It came into Hose's mind that the case was se-

43

rious. Jack was going to die. He never went to church, but perhaps the Sunday-school might count for something. He was only a Frenchman, after all, and Frenchmen had their own ways of doing things. He certainly ought to see some kind of a preacher before he went out of the wilderness. There was a Canadian priest in town that week, who had come down to see about getting up a church for the French people who worked in the mills. Perhaps Jack would like to talk with him.

His face lighted up at the proposal. He asked to have the room tidied up, and a clean shirt put on him, and the violin laid open in its case on a table beside the bed, and a few other preparations made for the visit. Then the visitor came, a tall, friendly, quiet-looking man about Jacques's age, with a smooth face and a long black cassock. The door was shut, and they were left alone together.

"I am comforted that you are come, *mon père*," said the sick man, "for I have the heavy heart. There is a secret that I have kept for many years. Sometimes I had almost forgotten that it must be told at the last; but now it is the time to speak.

I have a sin to confess—a sin of the most grievous, of the most unpardonable."

The listener soothed him with gracious words; spoke of the mercy that waits for all the penitent; urged him to open his heart without delay.

"Well, then, *mon père*, it is this that makes me fear to die. Long since, in Canada, before I came to this place, I have killed a man. It was—"

The voice stopped. The little round clock on the window-sill ticked very distinctly and rapidly, as if it were in a hurry.

"I will speak as short as I can. It was in the camp of 'Poléon Gautier, on the river St. Maurice. The big Baptiste Lacombe, that crazy boy who wants always to fight, he mocks me when I play, he snatches my violin, he goes to break him on the stove. There is a knife in my belt. I spring to Baptiste. I see no more what it is that I do. I cut him in the neck—once, twice. The blood flies out. He falls down. He cries, 'I die.' I grab my violin from the floor, quick; then I run to the woods. No one can catch me. A blanket, the axe, some food, I get from a hiding-place down the river. Then I travel,

travel, travel through the woods, how many days I know not, till I come here. No one knows me. I give myself the name Tremblay. I make the music for them. With my violin I live. I am happy. I forget. But it all returns to me—now—at the last. I have murdered. Is there a forgiveness for me, *mon père?*"

The priest's face had changed very swiftly at the mention of the camp on the St. Maurice. As the story went on, he grew strangely excited. His lips twitched. His hands trembled. At the end he sank on his knees, close by the bed, and looked into the countenance of the sick man, searching it as a forester searches in the undergrowth for a lost trail. Then his eyes lighted up as he found it.

"My son," said he, clasping the old fiddler's hand in his own, "you are Jacques Dellaire. And I—do you know me now?—I am Baptiste Lacombe. See those two scars upon my neck. But it was not death. You have not murdered. You have given the stroke that changed my heart. Your sin is forgiven—*and mine also*—by the mercy of God!"

The round clock ticked louder and louder. A

level ray from the setting sun—red gold—came in through the dusty window, and lay across the clasped hands on the bed. A white-throated sparrow, the first of the season, on his way to the woods beyond the St. Lawrence, whistled so clearly and tenderly that it seemed as if he were repeating to these two gray-haired exiles the name of their homeland. "*Sweet—sweet—Canada, Canada, Canada!*" But there was a sweeter sound than that in the quiet room.

It was the sound of the prayer which begins, in every language spoken by men, with the name of that Unseen One who rules over life's chances, and pities its discords, and tunes it back again into harmony. Yes, this prayer of the little children who are only learning how to play the first notes of life's music, turns to the great Master musician who knows it all and who loves to bring a melody out of every instrument that He has made; and it seems to lay the soul in His hands to play upon as He will, while it calls Him, *Our Father!*

·   ·   ·   ·   ·   ·   ·   ·

Some day, perhaps, you will go to the busy place

where Bytown used to be; and if you do, you must take the street by the river to the white wooden church of St. Jacques. It stands on the very spot where there was once a cabin with a curved roof. There is a gilt cross on the top of the church. The door is usually open, and the interior is quite gay with vases of china and brass, and paper flowers of many colours; but if you go through to the sacristy at the rear, you will see a brown violin hanging on the wall.

Père Baptiste, if he is there, will take it down and show it to you. He calls it a remarkable instrument —one of the best, of the most sweet.

But he will not let any one play upon it. He says it is a relic.

THE REWARD OF VIRTUE

THE REWARD OF VIRTUE

I

WHEN the good priest of St. Gérôme christened Patrick Mullarkey, he lent himself unconsciously to an innocent deception. To look at the name, you would think, of course, it belonged to an Irishman; the very appearance of it was equal to a certificate of membership in a Fenian society.

But in effect, from the turned-up toes of his *bottes sauvages* to the ends of his black mustache, the proprietor of this name was a Frenchman—Canadian French, you understand, and therefore even more proud and tenacious of his race than if he had been born in Normandy. Somewhere in his family tree there must have been a graft from the Green Isle. A wandering lumberman from County Kerry had drifted up the Saguenay into the Lake St. John region, and married the daughter of a *habitant*, and settled down to forget his own country and his father's house. But every visible trace of this infusion of new blood had vanished long ago, except the name; and the name itself was transformed on the lips of the St. Géromians. If you had heard them speak it in their pleasant droning accent,—"Patrique Moullarqué,"—you would have supposed that it was made in France. To have a guide with such a name as that was as good as being abroad.

Even when they cut it short and called him "Patte," as they usually did, it had a very foreign sound. Everything about him was in harmony with it; he spoke and laughed and sang and thought and felt in French—the French of two hundred years ago, the language of Samuel de Champlain and the Sieur de Monts, touched with a strong woodland flavour. In short, my guide, philosopher, and friend, Pat, did not have a drop of Irish in him, unless, perhaps, it was a certain—well, you shall judge for yourself, when you have heard this story of his virtue, and the way it was rewarded.

It was on the shore of the Lac à la Belle Rivière, fifteen miles back from St. Gérôme, that I came into the story, and found myself, as commonly happens in the real stories which life is always bringing out in periodical form, somewhere about the middle of the plot. But Patrick readily made me acquainted with what had gone before. Indeed, it is one of life's greatest charms as a story-teller that there is never any trouble about getting a brief résumé of the argument, and even a listener who arrives late is soon put into touch with the course of the narrative.

We had hauled our canoes and camp-stuff over the terrible road that leads to the lake, with much creaking and groaning of wagons, and complaining of men, who declared that the mud grew deeper and the hills steeper every year, and vowed their customary vow never to come that way again. At last our tents were pitched in a green copse of balsam trees, close beside the water. The delightful sense of peace and freedom descended upon our souls. Prosper and Ovide were cutting wood for the camp-fire; François was getting ready a brace of partridges for supper; Patrick and I were unpacking the provisions, arranging them conveniently for present use and future transportation.

"Here, Pat," said I, as my hand fell on a large square parcel—"here is some superfine tobacco that I got in Quebec for you and the other men on this trip. Not like the damp stuff you had last year—a little bad smoke and too many bad words. This is tobacco to burn—something quite particular, you understand. How does that please you?"

He had been rolling up a piece of salt pork in a cloth as I spoke, and courteously wiped his fingers on the outside of the bundle before he stretched out his hand to take the package of tobacco. Then he answered, with his unfailing politeness, but more solemnly than usual:

"A thousand thanks to m'sieu'. But this year I shall not have need of the good tobacco. It shall be for the others."

The reply was so unexpected that it almost took my breath away. For Pat, the steady smoker, whose pipes were as invariable as the precession of the equinoxes, to refuse his regular rations of the soothing weed was a thing unheard of. Could he be growing proud in his old age? Had he some secret supply of cigars concealed in his kit, which made him scorn the golden Virginia leaf? I demanded an explanation.

"But no, m'sieu'," he replied; "it is not that, most

assuredly. It is something entirely different—something very serious. It is a reformation that I commence. Does m'sieu' permit that I should inform him of it?"

Of course I permitted, or rather, warmly encouraged, the fullest possible unfolding of the tale; and while we sat among the bags and boxes, and the sun settled gently down behind the sharp-pointed firs across the lake, and the evening sky and the waveless lake glowed with a thousand tints of deepening rose and amber, Patrick put me in possession of the facts which had led to a moral revolution in his life.

"It was the Ma'm'selle Meelair, that young lady, —not very young, but active like the youngest,— the one that I conducted down the Grande Décharge to Chicoutimi last year, after you had gone away. She said that she knew m'sieu' intimately. No doubt you have a good remembrance of her?"

I admitted an acquaintance with the lady. She was the president of several societies for ethical agitation—a long woman, with short hair and eyeglasses and a great thirst for tea; not very good in a canoe, but always wanting to run the rapids and go into the dangerous places, and talking all the time. Yes; that must have been the one. She was not a bosom friend of mine, to speak accurately, but I remembered her well.

"Well, then, m'sieu'," continued Patrick, "it was this demoiselle who changed my mind about the smoking. But not in a moment, you understand; it was a work of four days, and she spoke much. .

"The first day it was at the Island House; we were trolling for ouananiche, and she was not pleased, for she lost many of the fish. I was smoking at the stern of the canoe, and she said that the tobacco was a filthy weed, that it grew in the devil's garden, and that it smelled bad, terribly bad, and that it made the air sick, and that even the pig would not eat it."

I could imagine Patrick's dismay as he listened to this dissertation; for in his way he was as sensitive as a woman, and he would rather have been upset in his canoe than have exposed himself to the reproach of offending any one of his patrons by unpleasant or unseemly conduct.

"What did you do then, Pat?" I asked.

"Certainly I put out the pipe—what could I do otherwise? But I thought that what the demoiselle Meelair has said was very strange, and not true—exactly; for I have often seen the tobacco grow, and it springs up out of the ground like the wheat or the beans, and it has beautiful leaves, broad and green, with sometimes a red flower at the top. Does the good God cause the filthy weeds to grow like that? Are they not all clean that He has made? The potato—it is not filthy. And the onion? It has a strong smell; but the demoiselle Meelair she ate much of the onion—when we were not at the Island House, but in the camp.

"And the smell of the tobacco—this is an affair of the taste. For me, I love it much; it is like a spice. When I come home at night to the camp-fire, where the boys are smoking, the smell of the pipes runs far out into the woods to salute me. It says, 'Here we are, Patrique; come in near to the fire.' The smell of the tobacco is more sweet than the smell of the fish. The pig loves it not, assuredly; but what then? I am not a pig. To me it is good,

good, good. Don't you find it like that, m'sieu'?"

I had to confess that in the affair of taste I sided with Patrick rather than with the pig. "Continue," I said—"continue, my boy. Miss Miller must have said more than that to reform you."

"Truly," replied Pat. "On the second day we were making the lunch at midday on the island below the first rapids. I smoked the pipe on a rock apart, after the collation. Mees Meelair comes to me, and says: 'Patrique, my man, do you comprehend that the tobacco is a poison? You are committing the murder of yourself.' Then she tells me many things—about the nicoline, I think she calls him: how he goes into the blood and into the bones and into the hair, and how quickly he will kill the cat. And she says, very strong, 'The men who smoke the tobacco shall die!'"

"That must have frightened you well, Pat. I suppose you threw away your pipe at once."

"But no, m'sieu'; this time I continue to smoke; for now it is Mees Meelair who comes near the pipe voluntarily, and it is not my offence. And I remember, while she is talking, the old bonhomme Michaud

58

at St. Gérôme. He is a capable man; when he was young he could carry a barrel of flour a mile without rest, and now that he has seventy-three years he yet keeps his force. And he smokes—it is astonishing how that old man smokes! All the day, except when he sleeps. If the tobacco is a poison, it is a poison of the slowest—like the tea or the coffee. For the cat it is quick—yes; but for the man it is long; and I am still young—only thirty-one.

"But the third day, m'sieu'—the third day was the worst. It was a day of sadness, a day of the bad chance. The demoiselle Meelair was not content but that we should leap the Rapide des Cèdres in canoe. It was rough, rough—all feather-white, and the big rock at the corner boiling like a kettle. But it is the ignorant who have the most of boldness. The demoiselle Meelair she was not solid in the canoe. She made a jump and a loud scream. I did my possible, but the sea was too high. We took in of the water about five buckets. We were very wet. After that we make the camp; and while I sit by the fire to dry my clothes I smoke for comfort.

"Mees Meelair she comes to me once more. 'Patrique,' she says with a sad voice, 'I am sorry that a nice man, so good, so brave, is married to a thing so bad, so sinful!' At first I am mad when I hear this, because I think she means Angélique, my wife; but immediately she goes on: 'You are married to the smoking. That is sinful; it is a wicked thing. Christians do not smoke. There is none of the tobacco in heaven. The men who use it cannot go there. Ah, Patrique, do you wish to go to the hell with your pipe?'"

"That was a close question," I commented; "your Miss Miller is a plain speaker. But what did you say when she asked you that?"

"I said, m'sieu'," replied Patrick, lifting his hand to his forehead, "that I must go where the good God pleased to send me, and that I would have much joy to go to the same place with our curé, the Père Morel, who is a great smoker. I am sure that the pipe of comfort is no sin to that holy man when he returns, some cold night, from the visiting of the sick — it is not sin, not more than the soft chair and the warm fire. It harms no one, and it makes quietness of mind. For me, when I see m'sieu' the curé sitting at the door of the *presbytère*, in the evening coolness, smoking the tobacco, very peaceful, and when he says to me, 'Good day, Patrique; will you have a pipeful?' I cannot think that is wicked —no!"

There was a warmth of sincerity in the honest fellow's utterance that spoke well for the character of the curé of St. Gérôme. The good word of a plain fisherman or hunter is worth more than a degree of doctor of divinity from a learned university.

I too had grateful memories of good men, faithful, charitable, wise, devout,—men before whose virtues my heart stood uncovered and reverent, men whose lives were sweet with self-sacrifice, and whose words were like stars of guidance to many souls,— and I had often seen these men solacing their toils and inviting pleasant, kindly thoughts with the pipe of peace. I wondered whether Miss Miller ever had the good fortune to meet any of these men. They were not members of the societies for ethical agitation, but they were profitable men to know. Their very presence was medicinal. It breathed patience and fidelity to duty, and a large, quiet friendliness.

"Well, then," I asked, "what did she say finally to turn you? What was her last argument? Come, Pat, you must make it a little shorter than she did."

"In five words, m'sieu', it was this: 'The tobacco causes the poverty.' The fourth day—you remind yourself of the long dead-water below the Rapide Gervais? It was there. All the day she spoke to me of the money that goes to the smoke. Two piastres the month. Twenty-four the year. Three hundred— yes, with the interest, more than three hundred in ten years! Two thousand piastres in the life of the man! But she comprehends well the arithmetic, that demoiselle Meelair; it was enormous! The big farmer Tremblay has not more money at the bank than that. Then she asks me if I have been at Quebec? No. If I would love to go? Of course, yes. For two years of the smoking we could go, the goodwife and me, to Quebec, and see the grand city, and the shops, and the many people, and the cathedral, and perhaps the theatre. And at the asylum of the orphans we could seek one of the little found children to bring home with us, to be our own; for m'sieu' knows it is the sadness of our house that we have no

child. But it was not Mees Meelair who said that—
no, she would not understand that thought."

Patrick paused for a moment, and rubbed his chin
reflectively. Then he continued:

"And perhaps it seems strange to you also,
m'sieu', that a poor man should be so hungry for
children. It is not so everywhere: not in America, I
hear. But it is so with us in Canada. I know not a
man so poor that he would not feel richer for a
child. I know not a man so happy that he would
not feel happier with a child in the house. It is the
best thing that the good God gives to us; something
to work for; something to play with. It makes a man
more gentle and more strong. And a woman,—her
heart is like an empty nest, if she has not a child. It
was the darkest day that ever came to Angélique
and me when our little baby flew away, four years
ago. But perhaps if we have not one of our own,
there is another somewhere, a little child of nobody,
that belongs to us, for the sake of the love of children. Jean Boucher, my wife's cousin, at St. Joseph
d'Alma, has taken two from the asylum. Two,
m'sieu', I assure you; for as soon as one was twelve

years old, he said he wanted a baby, and so he went back again and got another. That is what I should like to do."

"But, Pat," said I, "it is an expensive business, this raising of children. You should think twice about it."

"Pardon, m'sieu'," answered Patrick; "I think a hundred times and always the same way. It costs little more for three, or four, or five, in the house than for two. The only thing is the money for the journey to the city, the choice, the arrangement with the nuns. For that one must save. And so I have thrown away the pipe. I smoke no more. The money of the tobacco is for Quebec and for the little found child. I have already eighteen piastres and twenty sous in the old box of cigars on the chimney-piece at the house. This year will bring more. The winter after the next, if we have the good chance, we go to the city, the goodwife and me, and we come home with the little boy—or maybe the little girl. Does m'sieu' approve?"

"You are a man of virtue, Pat," said I; "and since you will not take your share of the tobacco on this trip, it shall go to the other men; but you shall have the money instead, to put into your box on the mantel-piece."

After supper that evening I watched him with some curiosity to see what he would do without his pipe. He seemed restless and uneasy. The other men sat around the fire, smoking; but Patrick was down at the landing, fussing over one of the canoes, which had been somewhat roughly handled on the road coming in. Then he began to tighten the tent-ropes, and hauled at them so vigorously that he loosened two of the stakes. Then he whittled the blade of his paddle for a while, and cut it an inch too short. Then he went into the men's tent, and in a few minutes the sound of snoring told that he had sought refuge in sleep at eight o'clock, without telling a single caribou story, or making any plans for the next day's sport.

II

FOR several days we lingered on the Lake of the Beautiful River, trying the fishing. We explored all the favourite meeting-places of the trout, at the mouths of the streams and in the cool spring-holes, but we did not have remarkable success. I am bound to say that Patrick was not at his best that year as a fisherman. He was as ready to work, as interested, as eager, as ever; but he lacked steadiness, persistence, patience. Some tranquillizing influence seemed to have departed from him. That placid confidence in the ultimate certainty of catching fish, which is one of the chief elements of good luck, was wanting. He did not appear to be able to sit still in the canoe. The mosquitoes troubled him terribly. He was just as anxious as a man could be to have me take plenty of the largest trout, but he was too much in a hurry. He even went so far as to say that he did not think I cast the fly as well as I did formerly, and that I was too slow in striking when the fish rose. He was distinctly a weaker man without his pipe, but his virtuous resolve held firm.

There was one place in particular that required very cautious angling. It was a spring-hole at the mouth of the Rivière du Milieu—an open space, about a hundred feet long and fifteen feet wide, in

the midst of the lily-pads, and surrounded on every
side by clear, shallow water. Here the great trout
assembled at certain hours of the day; but it was
not easy to get them. You must come up delicately
in the canoe, and make fast to a stake at the side of
the pool, and wait a long time for the place to get
quiet and the fish to recover from their fright and
come out from under the lily-pads. It had been our
custom to calm and soothe this expectant interval
with incense of the Indian weed, friendly to meditation and a foe of "Raw haste, half-sister to delay."
But this year Patrick could not endure the waiting.
After five minutes he would say:

"*But* the fishing is bad this season! There are
none of the big ones here at all. Let us try another
place. It will go better at the Rivière du Cheval,
perhaps."

There was only one thing that would really keep
him quiet, and that was a conversation about Quebec. The glories of that wonderful city entranced his
thoughts. He was already floating, in imagination,
with the vast throngs of people that filled its splendid streets, looking up at the stately houses and

churches with their glittering roofs of tin, and staring his fill at the magnificent shop-windows, where all the luxuries of the world were displayed. He had heard that there were more than a hundred shops— separate shops for all kinds of separate things: some for groceries, and some for shoes, and some for clothes, and some for knives and axes, and some for guns, and many shops where they sold only jewels—gold rings, and diamonds, and forks of pure silver. Was it not so?

He pictured himself, side by side with his goodwife, in the *salle à manger* of the Hôtel Richelieu, ordering their dinner from a printed bill of fare. Side by side they were walking on the Dufferin Terrace, listening to the music of the military band. Side by side they were watching the wonders of the play at the Théâtre de l'Étoile du Nord. Side by side they were kneeling before the gorgeous altar in the cathedral. And then they were standing silent, side by side, in the asylum of the orphans, looking at brown eyes and blue, at black hair and yellow curls, at fat legs and rosy cheeks and laughing mouths, while the Mother Superior showed off the

68

little boys and girls for them to choose. This affair of the choice was always a delightful difficulty, and here his fancy loved to hang in suspense, vibrating between rival joys.

Once, at the Rivière du Milieu, after considerable discourse upon Quebec, there was an interval of silence, during which I succeeded in hooking and playing a larger trout than usual. As the fish came up to the side of the canoe, Patrick netted him deftly, exclaiming with an abstracted air, "It is a boy, after all. I like that best."

Our camp was shifted, the second week, to the Grand Lac des Cèdres; and there we had extraordinary fortune with the trout: partly, I conjecture, because there was only one place to fish, and so Patrick's uneasy zeal could find no excuse for keeping me in constant motion all around the lake. But in the matter of weather we were not so happy. There is always a conflict in the angler's mind about the weather—a struggle between his desires as a man and his desires as a fisherman. This time our prayers for a good fishing season were granted at the expense of our suffering human nature. There was a conjunction in the zodiac of the signs of Aquarius and Pisces. It rained as easily, as suddenly, as penetratingly, as Miss Miller talked; but in between the showers the trout were very hungry.

One day, when we were paddling home to our tents among the birch trees, one of these unexpected storms came up; and Patrick, thoughtful of my comfort as ever, insisted on giving me his coat to put around my dripping shoulders. The paddling would serve instead of a coat for him, he said; it would keep him warm to his bones. As I slipped the garment over my back, something hard fell from one of the pockets into the bottom of the canoe. It was a brier-wood pipe.

"Aha! Pat," I cried; "what is this? You said you had thrown all your pipes away. How does this come in your pocket?"

"But, m'sieu'," he answered, "this is different. This is not the pipe pure and simple. It is a souvenir. It is the one you gave me two years ago on the Metabetchouan, when we got the big caribou. I could not reject this. I keep it always for the remembrance."

70

THE REWARD OF VIRTUE

At this moment my hand fell upon a small, square object in the other pocket of the coat. I pulled it out. It was a cake of Virginia leaf. Without a word, I held it up, and looked at Patrick. He began to explain eagerly:

"Yes, certainly, it is the tobacco, m'sieu'; but it is not for the smoke, as you suppose. It is for the virtue, for the self-victory. I call this my little piece of temptation. See, the edges are not cut. I smell it only; and when I think how it is good, then I speak to myself, 'But the little found child will be better!' It will last a long time, this little piece of temptation; perhaps until we have the boy at our house— or maybe the girl."

The conflict between the cake of Virginia leaf and Patrick's virtue must have been severe during the last ten days of our expedition; for we went down the Rivière des Écorces, and that is a tough trip, and full of occasions when consolation is needed. After a long, hard day's work cutting out an abandoned portage through the woods, or tramping miles over the incredibly shaggy hills to some outlying pond for a caribou, and lugging the saddle and hind quarters back to the camp, the evening pipe, after supper, seemed to comfort the men unspeakably. If their tempers had grown a little short under stress of fatigue and hunger, now they became cheerful and good-natured again. They sat on logs before the camp-fire, their stockinged feet stretched out to the blaze, and the puffs of smoke rose from their lips like tiny salutes to the comfortable flame, or like in-cense burned upon the altar of gratitude and con-tentment.

Patrick, I noticed about this time, liked to get on the leeward side of as many pipes as possible, and as near as he could to the smokers. He said that this kept away the mosquitoes. There he would sit, with the smoke drifting full in his face, both hands in his pockets, talking about Quebec, and debating the comparative merits of a boy or a girl as an addition to his household.

But the great trial of his virtue was yet to come. The main object of our trip down the River of Barks—the *terminus ad quem* of the expedition, so to speak—was a bear. Now the bear as an object of the chase, at least in Canada, is one of the most illusory of phantoms. The manner of hunting is simple. It consists in walking about through the woods, or paddling along a stream, until you meet a bear; then you try to shoot him. This would seem to be, as the Rev. Mr. Leslie called his book against the deists of the eighteenth century, "A Short and Easie Method." But in point of fact there are two principal difficulties. The first is that you never find the bear when and where you are looking for him. The second is that the bear sometimes finds you when— but you shall see how it happened to us.

We had hunted the whole length of the River of Barks with the utmost pains and caution, never going out, even to pick blueberries, without having the rifle at hand, loaded for the expected encounter. Not one bear had we met. It seemed as if the whole ursine tribe must have emigrated to Labrador.

At last we came to the mouth of the river, where it empties into Lake Kenogami, in a comparatively civilized country, with several farm-houses in full view on the opposite bank. It was not a promising place for the chase; but the river ran down with a little fall and a lively, cheerful rapid into the lake, and it was a capital spot for fishing. So we left the rifle in the case, and took a canoe and a rod, and went down, on the last afternoon, to stand on the point of rocks at the foot of the rapid, and cast the fly.

We caught half a dozen good trout; but the sun was still hot, and we concluded to wait awhile for the evening fishing. So we turned the canoe bottom up among the bushes on the shore, stored the trout away in the shade beneath it, and sat down in a convenient place among the stones to have another chat about Quebec. We had just passed the jewelry-shops, and were preparing to go to the asylum of the orphans, when Patrick put his hand on my shoulder with a convulsive grip, and pointed up the stream.

There was a huge bear, like a very big, wicked, black sheep with a pointed nose, making his way down the shore. He shambled along lazily and un-concernedly, as if his bones were loosely tied to-gether in a bag of fur. It was the most indifferent and disconnected gait that I ever saw. Nearer and nearer he sauntered, while we sat as still as if we had been paralyzed. And the gun was in its case at the tent!

How the bear knew this I cannot tell; but know it he certainly did, fo₁ he kept on until he reached the canoe, sniffed at it suspiciously, thrust his sharp nose under it, and turned it over with a crash that knocked two holes in the bottom, ate the fish, licked his chops, stared at us for a few moments without the slightest appearance of gratitude, made up his mind that he did not like our personal appearance, and then loped leisurely up the mountain-side. We could hear him cracking the underbrush long after he was lost to sight.

Patrick looked at me and sighed. I said nothing. The French language, as far as I knew it, seemed trifling and inadequate. It was a moment when nothing could do any good except the consolations of philosophy, or a pipe. Patrick pulled the brier-wood from his pocket; then he took out the cake of Virginia leaf, looked at it, smelled it, shook his head, and put it back again. His face was as long as his arm. He stuck the cold pipe into his mouth, and pulled away at it for a while in silence. Then his countenance began to clear, his mouth relaxed, he broke into a laugh.

"Sacred bear!" he cried, slapping his knee; "sacred beast of the world! What a day of the good chance for her, *hé!* But she was glad, I suppose. Perhaps she has some cubs, *hé? Bajette!*"

III

THIS was the end of our hunting and fishing for that year. We spent the next two days in voyaging through a half-dozen small lakes and streams, in a farming country, on our way home. I observed that Patrick kept his souvenir pipe between his lips a good deal of the time, and puffed at vacancy. It seemed to soothe him. In his conversation he dwelt with peculiar satisfaction on the thought of the money in the cigar-box on the mantel-piece at St. Gérôme. Eighteen piastres and twenty sous already! And with the addition to be made from the tobacco not smoked during the past month, it would amount to more than twenty-three piastres; and all as safe in the cigar-box as if it were in the bank at Chicoutimi! That reflection seemed to fill the empty pipe with fragrance. It was a Barmecide smoke; but the fumes of it were potent, and their invisible wreaths framed the most enchanting visions of tall towers, gray walls, glittering windows, crowds of people, regiments of soldiers, and the laughing eyes of a little boy—or was it a little girl?

When we came out of the mouth of La Belle Rivière, the broad blue expanse of Lake St. John spread before us, calm and bright in the radiance of the sinking sun. In a curve on the left, eight miles away, sparkled the slender steeple of the church of St. Gérôme. A thick column of smoke rose from somewhere in its neighbourhood. "It is on the beach," said the men; "the boys of the village accustom themselves to burn the rubbish there for a bonfire." But as our canoes danced lightly forward over the waves and came nearer to the place, it was evident that the smoke came from the village itself. It was a conflagration, but not a general one; the houses were too scattered and the day too still for a fire to spread. What could it be? Perhaps the blacksmith shop, perhaps the bakery, perhaps the old tumble-down barn of the little Tremblay? It was not a large fire, that was certain. But where was it precisely?

The question, becoming more and more anxious, was answered when we arrived at the beach. A handful of boys, eager to be the bearers of news, had spied us far off, and ran down to the shore to meet us.

"Patrique! Patrique!" they shouted in English, to make their importance as great as possible in my eyes. "Come 'ome kveek; yo' 'ouse ees hall burn'!"

"W'at!" cried Patrick. "*Monjee!*" And he drove the canoe ashore, leaped out, and ran up the bank toward the village as if he were mad. The other men followed him, leaving me with the boys to unload the canoes and pull them up on the sand, where the waves would not chafe them.

This took some time, and the boys helped me willingly. "Eet ees not need to 'urry, m'sieu'," they assured me; "dat 'ouse to Patrique Moullarqué ees hall burn' seence t'ree hour. Not'ing lef' bot de hash."

As soon as possible, however, I piled up the stuff, covered it with one of the tents, and leaving it in charge of the steadiest of the boys, took the road to the village and the site of the Maison Mullarkey.

It had vanished completely: the walls of squared logs were gone; the low, curved roof had fallen; the door-step with the morning-glory vines climbing up beside it had sunken out of sight; nothing remained but the dome of the clay oven at the back of the house, and a heap of smouldering embers.

Patrick sat beside his wife on a flat stone that had formerly supported the corner of the porch. His shoulder was close to Angélique's—so close that it looked almost as if he must have had his arm around her a moment before I came up. His passion and grief had calmed themselves down now, and he was quite tranquil. In his left hand he held the cake of Virginia leaf, in his right a knife. He was cutting off delicate slivers of the tobacco, which he rolled together with a circular motion between his palms. Then he pulled his pipe from his pocket and filled the bowl with great deliberation.

"What a misfortune!" I cried. "The pretty house

79

is gone. I am so sorry, Patrick. And the box of money on the mantel-piece, that is gone, too, I fear —all your savings. What a terrible misfortune! How did it happen?"

"I cannot tell," he answered rather slowly. "It is the good God. And he has left me my Angélique. Also, m'sieu', you see"—here he went over to the pile of ashes, and pulled out a fragment of charred wood with a live coal at the end—"you see"—puff, puff—"he has given me"—puff, puff—"a light for my pipe again"—puff, puff, puff!

The fragrant, friendly smoke was pouring out now in full volume. It enwreathed his head like drifts of cloud around the rugged top of a mountain at sunrise. I could see that his face was spreading into a smile of ineffable contentment.

"My faith!" said I, "how can you be so cheerful? Your house is in ashes; your money is burned up; the voyage to Quebec, the visit to the asylum, the little orphan—how can you give it all up so easily?"

"Well," he replied, taking the pipe from his mouth, with fingers curling around the bowl, as if

"He has given me . . . a light for my pipe."

they loved to feel that it was warm once more—
"well, then, it would be more hard, I suppose, to
give it up not easily. And then, for the house, we
shall build a new one this fall; the neighbours will
help. And for the voyage to Quebec—without that
we may be happy. And as regards the little orphan,
I will tell you frankly"—here he went back to his
seat upon the flat stone, and settled himself with an
air of great comfort beside his partner—"I tell you,
in confidence, Angélique demands that I prepare a
particular furniture at the new house. Yes, it is a
cradle; but it is not for an orphan."

IV

It was late in the following summer when I came
back again to St. Gérôme. The golden-rods and the
asters were all in bloom along the village street; and
as I walked down it the broad golden sunlight of the
short afternoon seemed to glorify the open road and
the plain square houses with a careless, homely rap-
ture of peace. The air was softly fragrant with the
odour of balm of Gilead. A yellow warbler sang from

a little clump of elder-bushes, tinkling out his contented song like a chime of tiny bells, "*Sweet—sweet
—sweet—sweeter—sweeter—sweetest!*"

There was the new house, a little farther back
from the road than the old one; and in the place
where the heap of ashes had lain, a primitive garden,
with marigolds and lupines and zinnias all abloom.
And there was Patrick, sitting on the door-step,
smoking his pipe in the cool of the day. Yes; and
there, on a many-coloured counterpane spread beside
him, an infant joy of the house of Mullarkey was
sucking her thumb, while her father was humming
the words of an old slumber-song:

> *Sainte Marguerite,*
> *Veillez ma petite!*
> *Endormez ma p'tite enfant*
> *Jusqu'à l'âge de quinze ans!*
> *Quand elle aura quinze ans passé*
> *Il faudra la marier*
> *Avec un p'tit bonhomme*
> *Que viendra de Rome.*

"Hola! Patrick," I cried; "good luck to you! Is
it a girl or a boy?"

"*Salut!* m'sieu'," he answered, jumping up and waving his pipe. "It is a girl *and* a boy!"

Sure enough, as I entered the door, I beheld Angélique rocking the other half of the reward of virtue in the new cradle.

A BRAVE HEART

A BRAVE HEART

"That was truly his name, m'sieu'—Raoul Vaillant-cœur—a name of the fine sound, is it not? You like that word,—a valiant heart,—it pleases you, eh! The man who calls himself by such a name as that ought to be a brave fellow, a veritable hero? Well, perhaps. But I know an Indian who is called Le Blanc; that means white. And a white man who is called Lenoir; that means black. It is very droll, this affair of the names. It is like the lottery."

Silence for a few moments, broken only by the ripple of water under the bow of the canoe, the persistent patter of the rain all around us, and the *slish, slish* of the paddle with which Ferdinand, my Canadian voyageur, was pushing the birch-bark down the lonely length of Lac Moïse. I knew that there was one of his stories on the way. But I must keep still to get it. A single ill-advised comment, a word that would raise a question of morals or social philosophy, might switch the narrative off the track into a swamp of abstract discourse in which Ferdinand would lose himself. Presently the voice behind me began again.

"But that word *vaillant*, m'sieu'; with us in Canada it does not mean always the same as with you. Sometimes we use it for something that sounds big, but does little; a gun that goes off with a terrible crack, but shoots not straight nor far. When a man is like that he is *fanfaron*, he shows off well, but— well, you shall judge for yourself, when you hear what happened between this man Vaillantcœur and his friend Prosper Leclère at the building of the stone tower of the church at Abbéville. You remind yourself of that grand church with the tall tower—yes? With permission I am going to tell you what passed when that was made. And you shall decide whether there was truly a brave heart in the story, or not; and if it went with the name."

Thus the tale began, in the vast solitude of the northern forest, among the granite peaks of the ancient Laurentian Mountains, on a lake that knew no human habitation save the Indian's wigwam or the fisherman's tent.

How it rained that day! The dark clouds had

collapsed upon the hills in shapeless folds. The waves of the lake were beaten flat by the lashing strokes of the storm. Quivering sheets of watery gray were driven before the wind; and broad curves of silver bullets danced before them as they swept over the surface. All around the homeless shores the evergreen trees seemed to hunch their backs and crowd closer together in patient misery. Not a bird had the heart to sing; only the loon—storm-lover— laughed his crazy challenge to the elements, and mocked us with his long-drawn maniac scream.

It seemed as if we were a thousand miles from everywhere and everybody. Cities, factories, libraries, colleges, law-courts, theatres, palaces,—what had we dreamed of these things? They were far off, in another world. We had slipped back into a primitive life. Ferdinand was telling me the naked story of human love and human hate, even as it has been told from the beginning.

I cannot tell it just as he did. There was a charm in his speech too quick for the pen; a woodland savour not to be found in any ink for sale in the shops. I must tell it in my way, as he told it in his.

But at all events, nothing that makes any difference shall go into the translation unless it was in the original. This is Ferdinand's story. If you care for the real thing, here it is.

I

THERE were two young men in Abbéville who were easily the cocks of the woodland walk. Their standing rested on the fact that they were the strongest men in the parish. Strength is the thing that counts, when people live on the edge of the wilderness. These two were well known all through the country between Lake St. John and Chicoutimi as men of great capacity. Either of them could shoulder a barrel of flour and walk off with it as lightly as a common man would carry a side of bacon. There was not a half-pound of difference between them in ability. But there was a great difference in their looks and in their way of doing things.

Raoul Vaillantcœur was the biggest and the handsomest man in the village; nearly six feet tall, straight as a fir tree, and black as a bull-moose in

December. He had natural force enough and to spare. Whatever he did was done by sheer power of back and arm. He could send a canoe up against the heaviest water, provided he did not get mad and break his paddle—which he often did. He had more muscle than he knew how to use.

Prosper Leclère did not have so much, but he knew better how to handle it. He never broke his paddle—unless it happened to be a bad one, and then he generally had another all ready in the canoe. He was at least four inches shorter than Vaillantcœur; broad shoulders, long arms, light hair, gray eyes; not a handsome fellow, but pleasant-looking and very quiet. What he did was done more than half with his head.

He was the kind of a man that never needs more than one match to light a fire.

But Vaillantcœur—well, if the wood was wet he might use a dozen, and when the blaze was kindled, as like as not he would throw in the rest of the box.

Now, these two men had been friends and were changed into rivals. At least that was the way that one of them looked at it. And most of the people in

91

the parish seemed to think that was the right view.

It was a strange thing, and not altogether satisfactory to the public mind, to have *two* strongest men in the village. The question of comparative standing in the community ought to be raised and settled in the usual way. Raoul was perfectly willing, and at times (commonly on Saturday nights) very eager. But Prosper was not.

"No," he said, one March night, when he was boiling maple-sap in the sugar-bush with little Ovide Rossignol (who had a lyric passion for holding the coat while another man was fighting)—"no, for what shall I fight with Raoul? As boys we have played together. Once, in the rapids of the Belle Rivière, when I have fallen in the water, I think he has saved my life. He was stronger, then, than me. I am always a friend to him. If I beat him now, am I stronger? No, but weaker. And if he beats me, what is the sense of that? Certainly I shall not like it. What is to gain?"

Down in the store of old Girard, that night, Vaillantcœur was holding forth after a different fashion. He stood among the cracker-boxes and flour-barrels, with a background of shelves laden with bright-coloured calicoes, and a line of tin pails hanging overhead, and stated his view of the case with vigour. He even pulled off his coat and rolled up his shirt-sleeve to show the knotty arguments with which he proposed to clinch his opinion.

"That Leclère," said he, "that little Prosper Leclère! He thinks himself one of the strongest—a fine fellow! But I tell you he is a coward. If he is clever? Yes. But he is a poltroon. He knows well that I can flatten him out like a *crêpe* in the frying-pan. But he is afraid. He has not as much courage as the musk-rat. You stamp on the bank. He dives. He swims away. Bah!"

"How about that time he cut loose the jam of logs in the Rapide des Cèdres?" said old Girard from his corner.

Vaillantcœur's black eyes sparkled and he twirled his mustache fiercely. "*Saprie!*" he cried, "that was nothing! Any man with an axe can cut a log. But to fight—that is another affair. That demands the brave heart. The strong man who will not fight is a coward. Some day I will put him through the mill—

you shall see what that small Leclère is made of.
Sacrédam!"

Of course, affairs had not come to this pass all
at once. It was a long history, beginning with the
time when the two boys had played together, and
Raoul was twice as strong as the other, and was
very proud of it. Prosper did not care; it was all
right so long as they had a good time. But then
Prosper began to do things better and better. Raoul
did not understand it; he was jealous. Why should
he not always be the leader? He had more force.
Why should Prosper get ahead? Why should he
have better luck at the fishing and the hunting and
the farming? It was by some trick. There was no
justice in it.

Raoul was not afraid of anything but death; and
whatever he wanted, he thought he had a right to
have. But he did not know very well how to get it.
He would start to chop a log just at the spot where
there was a big knot.

He was the kind of a man that sets hare-snares
on a caribou-trail, and then curses his luck because
he catches nothing.

But to fight—that is another affair.

Besides, whatever he did, he was always thinking most about beating somebody else. But Prosper cared most for doing the thing as well as he could. If any one else could beat him—well, what difference did it make? He would do better the next time.

If he had a log to chop, he looked it all over for a clear place before he began. What he wanted was, not to make the chips fly, but to get the wood split.

You are not to suppose that the one man was a saint and a hero, and the other a fool and a ruffian. No; that sort of thing happens only in books. People in Abbéville were not made on that plan. They were both plain men. But there was a difference in their hearts; and out of that difference grew all the trouble.

It was hard on Vaillantcœur, of course, to see Leclère going ahead, getting rich, clearing off the mortgage on his farm, laying up money with the notary Bergeron, who acted as banker for the parish—it was hard to look on at this, while he himself stood still, or even slipped back a little, got into debt, had to sell a bit of the land that his father left him. There must be some cheating about it.

But this was not the hardest morsel to swallow. The great thing that stuck in his crop was the idea that the little Prosper, whom he could have whipped so easily, and whom he had protected so loftily, when they were boys, now stood just as high as he did as a capable man—perhaps even higher. Why was it that when the Price Brothers, down at Chicoutimi, had a good lumber-job up in the woods on the Belle Rivière, they made Leclère the boss, instead of Vaillantcœur? Why did the curé Villeneuve choose Prosper, and not Raoul, to steady the strain of the biggest pole when they were setting up the derrick for the building of the new church?

It was rough, rough! The more Raoul thought of it, the rougher it seemed. The fact that it was a man who had once been his *protégé*, and still insisted on being his best friend, did not make it any smoother. Would you have liked it any better on that account? I am not telling you how it ought to have been, I am telling you how it was. This isn't

Vaillantcœur's account-book; it's his story. You must strike your balances as you go along.

And all the time, you see, he felt sure that he was a stronger man and a braver man than Prosper. He was hungry to prove it in the only way that he could understand. The sense of rivalry grew into a passion of hatred, and the hatred shaped itself into a blind, headstrong desire to fight. Everything that Prosper did well, seemed like a challenge; every success that he had was as hard to bear as an insult. All the more, because Prosper seemed unconscious of it. He refused to take offence, went about his work quietly and cheerfully, turned off hard words with a joke, went out of his way to show himself friendly and good-natured. In reality, of course, he knew well enough how matters stood. But he was resolved not to show that he knew, if he could help it; and in any event, not to be one of the two that are needed to make a quarrel.

He felt very strangely about it. There was a presentiment in his heart that he did not dare to shake off. It seemed as if this conflict were one that would threaten the happiness of his whole life. He still kept his old feeling of attraction to Raoul, the memory of the many happy days they had spent together; and though the friendship, of course, could never again be what it had been, there was something of it left, at least on Prosper's side. To struggle with this man, strike at his face, try to maim and disfigure him, roll over and over on the ground with him, like two dogs tearing each other,—the thought was hateful. His gorge rose at it. He would never do it, unless to save his life. Then? Well, then, God must be his judge.

So it was that these two men stood against each other in Abbéville. Just as strongly as Raoul was set to get into a fight, just so strongly was Prosper set to keep out of one. It was a trial of strength between two passions,—the passion of friendship and the passion of fighting.

Two or three things happened to put an edge on Raoul's hunger for an out-and-out fight.

The first was the affair at the shanty on Lac des Caps. The wood-choppers, like sailors, have a way of putting a new man through a few tricks to initiate him into the camp. Leclère was bossing the job, with a gang of ten men from St. Raymond under him. Vaillantcœur had just driven a team in over the snow with a load of provisions, and was lounging around the camp as if it belonged to him. It was Sunday afternoon, the regular time for fun, but no one dared to take hold of him. He looked too big. He expressed his opinion of the camp.

"No fun in this shanty, *hé?* I suppose that little Leclère he makes you others work, and say your prayers, and then, for the rest, you can sleep. *Hé!* Well, I am going to make a little fun for you, my boys. Come, Prosper, get your hat, if you are able to climb a tree."

He snatched the hat from the table by the stove and ran out into the snow. In front of the shanty a good-sized birch, tall, smooth, very straight, was still standing. He went up the trunk like a bear.

But there was a dead balsam that had fallen against the birch and lodged on the lower branches. It was barely strong enough to bear the weight of a light man. Up this slanting ladder Prosper ran quickly in his moccasined feet, snatched the hat from Raoul's teeth as he swarmed up the trunk, and ran down again. As he neared the ground, the balsam, shaken from its lodgement, cracked and fell. Raoul was left up the tree, perched among the branches, out of breath. Luck had set the scene for the lumberman's favourite trick.

"Chop him down! chop him down!" was the cry; and a trio of axes were twanging against the birch tree, while the other men shouted and laughed and pelted the tree with ice to keep the prisoner from climbing down.

Prosper neither shouted nor chopped, but he grinned a little as he watched the tree quiver and shake, and heard the rain of "*sacrés!*" and "*maudits!*" that came out of the swaying top. He grinned —until he saw that a half-dozen more blows would fell the birch right on the roof of the shanty.

"Are you crazy?" he cried, as he picked up an axe; "you know nothing how to chop. You kill a man. You smash the *cabane*. Let go!" He shoved one of the boys away and sent a few mighty cuts into the side of the birch that was farthest from the cabin; then two short cuts on the other side; the tree shivered, staggered, cracked, and swept in a great arc toward the deep snow-drift by the brook.

As the top swung earthward, Raoul jumped clear of the crashing branches and landed safely in the feather-bed of snow, buried up to his neck. Nothing was to be seen of him but his head, like some new kind of fire-work—sputtering bad words.

Well, this was the first thing that put an edge on Vaillantcœur's hunger to fight. No man likes to be chopped down by his friend, even if the friend does it for the sake of saving him from being killed by a fall on the shanty-roof. It is easy to forget that part of it. What you remember is the grin.

The second thing that made it worse was the bad chance that both of these men had to fall in love with the same girl. Of course there were other girls in the village beside Marie Antoinette Girard— plenty of them, and good girls, too. But somehow or other, when they were beside her, neither Raoul nor Prosper cared to look at any of them, but only at 'Toinette. Her eyes were so much darker and her cheeks so much more red—bright as the berries of the mountain-ash in September. Her hair hung down to her waist on Sunday in two long braids, brown and shiny like a ripe hazelnut; and her voice when she laughed made the sound of water tumbling over little stones.

No one knew which of the two lovers she liked best. At school it was certainly Raoul, because he was bigger and bolder. When she came back from her year in the convent at Roberval it was certainly Prosper, because he could talk better and had read more books. He had a volume of songs full of love and romance, and knew most of them by heart. But this did not last forever. 'Toinette's manners had been polished at the convent, but her ideas were still those of her own people. She never thought that knowledge of books could take the place of strength, in the real battle of life. She was a brave girl, and she felt sure in her heart that the man of the most courage must be the best man after all.

For a while she appeared to persuade herself that it was Prosper, beyond a doubt, and always took his part when the other girls laughed at him. But this was not altogether a good sign. When a girl really loves, she does not talk, she acts. The current of opinion and gossip in the village was too strong for her. By the time of the affair of the "chopping-down" at Lac des Caps, her heart was swinging to and fro like a pendulum. One week she would walk home from mass with Raoul. The next week she would loiter in the front yard on a Saturday evening and talk over the gate with Prosper, until her father called her into the shop to wait on customers.

It was in one of these talks that the pendulum seemed to make its last swing and settle down to its resting-place. Prosper was telling her of the good crops of sugar that he had made from his maple grove.

"The profit will be large—more than sixty piastres—and with that I shall buy at Chicoutimi a new four-wheeler, of the finest, a veritable wedding-carriage—if you—if I—'Toinette? Shall we ride together?"

His left hand clasped hers as it lay on the gate. His right arm stole over the low picket fence and went around the shoulder that leaned against the gate-post. The road was quite empty, the night already dark. He could feel her warm breath on his neck as she laughed.

"If you! If I! If what? Why so many ifs in this fine speech? Of whom is the wedding for which this new carriage is to be bought? Do you know what Raoul Vaillantcœur has said? 'No more wedding in this parish till I have thrown the little Prosper over my shoulder!'"

As she said this, laughing, she turned closer to the fence and looked up, so that a curl on her forehead brushed against his cheek.

"*Batêche!* Who told you he said that?"

"I heard him, myself."

"Where?"

"In the store, two nights ago. But it was not for the first time. He said it when we came from the church together, it will be four weeks to-morrow."

"What did you say to him?"

"I told him perhaps he was mistaken. The next wedding might be after the little Prosper had measured the road with the back of the longest man in Abbéville."

The laugh had gone out of her voice now. She was speaking eagerly, and her bosom rose and fell with quick breaths. But Prosper's right arm had dropped from her shoulder, and his hand gripped the fence as he straightened up.

"'Toinette!" he cried, "that was bravely said. And I could do it. Yes, I know I could do it. But, *mon Dieu,* what shall I say? Three years now, he has pushed me, every one has pushed me, to fight. And you—but I cannot. I am not capable of it."

The girl's hand lay in his as cold and still as a stone. She was silent for a moment, and then asked, coldly, "Why not?"

"Why not? Because of the old friendship. Because he pulled me out of the river long ago. Because I am still his friend. Because now he hates me too much. Because it would be a black fight. Because shame and evil would come of it, whoever won. That is what I fear, 'Toinette!"

Her hand slipped suddenly away from his. She stepped back from the gate.

"*Tiens!* You have fear, Monsieur Leclère! Truly? I had not thought of that. It is strange. For so strong a man it is a little stupid to be afraid. Goodnight. I hear my father calling me. Perhaps some one in the store who wants to be served. You must tell me again what you are going to do with the new carriage. Good-night!"

She was laughing again. But it was a different laughter. Prosper, at the gate, did not think it sounded like the running of a brook over the stones. No, it was more the noise of the dry branches that knock together in the wind. He did not hear the sigh that came as she shut the door of the house, nor see how slowly she walked through the passage into the store.

II

THERE seemed to be a great many rainy Saturdays that spring; and in the early summer the trade in Girard's store was so brisk that it appeared to need all the force of the establishment to attend to it. The gate of the front yard had no more strain put upon its hinges. It fell into a stiff propriety of opening and shutting, at the touch of people who understood that a gate was made merely to pass through, not to lean upon.

That summer Vaillantcœur had a new hat—a

black and shiny beaver—and a new red-silk cravat.
They looked fine on Corpus Christi day, when he
and 'Toinette walked together as fiancées.

You would have thought he would have been content with that. Proud, he certainly was. He stepped
like the curé's big rooster with the topknot—almost
as far up in the air as he did along the ground; and
he held his chin high, as if he liked to look at things
over his nose.

But he was not satisfied all the way through. He
thought more of beating Prosper than of getting
'Toinette. And he was not quite sure that he had
beaten him yet.

Perhaps the girl still liked Prosper a little. Perhaps she still thought of his romances, and his
chansons, and his fine, smooth words, and missed
them. Perhaps she was too silent and dull sometimes, when she walked with Raoul; and sometimes
she laughed too loud when he talked, more at him
than with him. Perhaps those St. Raymond fellows
still remembered the way his head stuck out of that
cursed snow-drift, and joked about it, and said how
clever and quick the little Prosper was. Perhaps—

ah, *maudit!* a thousand times perhaps! And only one way to settle them, the old way, the sure way, and all the better now because 'Toinette must be on his side. She must understand for sure that the bravest man in the parish had chosen her.

That was the summer of the building of the grand stone tower of the church. The men of Abbéville did it themselves, with their own hands, for the glory of God. They were keen about that, and the curé was the keenest of them all. No sharing of that glory with workmen from Quebec, if you please! Abbéville was only forty years old, but they already understood the glory of God quite as well there as at Quebec, without doubt. They could build their own tower, perfectly, and they would. Besides, it would cost less.

Vaillantcœur was the chief carpenter. He attended to the affair of beams and timbers. Leclère was the chief mason. He directed the affair of dressing the stones and laying them. That required a very careful head, you understand, for the tower must be straight. In the floor a little crookedness did not matter; but in the wall—that might be serious. People have been killed by a falling tower. Of course, if they were going into church, they would be sure of heaven. But then think—what a disgrace for Abbéville!

Every one was glad that Leclère bossed the raising of the tower. They admitted that he might not be brave, but he was assuredly careful. Vaillantcœur alone grumbled, and said the work went too slowly, and even swore that the sockets for the beams were too shallow, or else too deep, it made no difference which. That *bête* Prosper made trouble always by his poor work. But the friction never came to a blaze; for the curé was pottering about the tower every day and all day long, and a few words from him would make a quarrel go off in smoke.

"Softly, my boys!" he would say; "work smooth and you work fast. The logs in the river run well when they run all the same way. But when two logs cross each other, on the same rock—psst! a jam! The whole drive is hung up! Do not run crossways, my children."

The walls rose steadily, straight as a steamboat pipe—ten, twenty, thirty, forty feet; it was time to put in the two cross-girders, lay the floor of the belfry, finish off the stonework, and begin the pointed wooden spire. The curé had gone to Quebec that very day to buy the shining plates of tin for the roof, and a beautiful cross of gilt for the pinnacle.

Leclère was in front of the tower putting on his overalls. Vaillantcœur came up, swearing mad. Three or four other workmen were standing about.

"Look here, you Leclère," said he, "I tried one of the cross-girders yesterday afternoon and it would n't go. The templet on the north is crooked—crooked as your teeth. We had to let the girder down again. I suppose we must trim it off some way, to get a level bearing, and make the tower weak, just to match your *sacré* bad work, eh?"

"Well," said Prosper, pleasant and quiet enough, "I'm sorry for that, Raoul. Perhaps I could put that templet straight, or perhaps the girder might be a little warped and twisted, eh? What? Suppose we measure it."

Sure enough, they found the long timber was not half seasoned and had corkscrewed itself out of shape at least three inches. Vaillantcœur sat on the sill of the doorway and did not even look at them while they were measuring. When they called out to him what they had found, he strode over to them.

"It's a dam' lie," he said, sullenly. "Prosper Leclère, you slipped the string. None of your *sacré* cheating! I have enough of it already. Will you fight, you cursed sneak?"

Prosper's face went gray, like the mortar in the trough. His fists clenched and the cords on his neck stood out as if they were ropes. He breathed hard. But he only said three words:

"No! Not here."

"Not here? Why not? There is room. The curé is away. Why not here?"

"It is the house of *le bon Dieu*. Can we build it in hate?"

"*Polisson!* You make an excuse. Then come to Girard's, and fight there."

Again Prosper held in for a moment, and spoke three words:

"No! Not now."

"Not now? But when, you heart of a hare? Will

you sneak out of it until you turn gray and die? When will you fight, little musk-rat?"

"When I have forgotten. When I am no more your friend."

Prosper picked up his trowel and went into the tower. Raoul bad-worded him and every stone of his building from foundation to cornice, and then went down the road to get a bottle of cognac.

An hour later he came back breathing out threatenings and slaughter, strongly flavoured with raw spirits. Prosper was working quietly on the top of the tower, at the side away from the road. He saw nothing until Raoul, climbing up by the ladders on the inside, leaped on the platform and rushed at him like a crazy lynx.

"Now!" he cried, "no hole to hide in here, rat! I'll squeeze the lies out of you."

He gripped Prosper by the head, thrusting one thumb into his eye, and pushing him backward on the scaffolding.

Blinded, half maddened by the pain, Prosper thought of nothing but to get free. He swung his long arm upward and landed a heavy blow on

Raoul's face that dislocated the jaw; then twisting himself downward and sideways, he fell in toward the wall. Raoul plunged forward, stumbled, let go his hold, and pitched out from the tower, arms spread, clutching the air.

Forty feet straight down! A moment — or was it an eternity? — of horrible silence. Then the body struck the rough stones at the foot of the tower with a thick, soft dunt, and lay crumpled up among them, without a groan, without a movement.

When the other men, who had hurried up the ladders in terror, found Leclère, he was peering over the edge of the scaffold, wiping the blood from his eyes, trying to see down.

"I have killed him," he muttered, "my friend! He is smashed to death. I am a murderer. Let me go. I must throw myself down!"

They had hard work to hold him back. As they forced him down the ladders he trembled like a poplar.

But Vaillantcœur was not dead. No; it was incredible—to fall forty feet and not be killed—they talk of it yet all through the valley of the Lake St.

John—it was a miracle! But Vaillantcœur had broken only a nose, a collar-bone, and two ribs—for one like him that was but a *bagatelle*. A good doctor from Chicoutimi, a few months of nursing, and he would be on his feet again, almost as good a man as he had ever been.

It was Leclère who put himself in charge of this.

"It is my affair," he said—"my fault! It was not a fair place to fight. Why did I strike? I must attend to this bad work."

"*Mais, sacré bleu!*" they answered, "how could you help it? He forced you. You did not want to be killed. That would be a little too much."

"No," he persisted, "this is my affair. Girard, you know my money is with the notary. There is plenty. Raoul has not enough, perhaps not any. But he shall want nothing—you understand—nothing! It is my affair, all that he needs—but you shall not tell him—no! That is all."

Prosper had his way. But he did not see Vaillantcœur after he was carried home and put to bed in his cabin. Even if he had tried to do so, it would have been impossible. He could not see anybody.

One of his eyes was entirely destroyed. The inflammation spread to the other, and all through the autumn he lay in his house, drifting along the edge of blindness, while Raoul lay in his house slowly getting well.

The curé went from one house to the other, but he did not carry any messages between them. If any were sent one way they were not received. And the other way, none were sent. Raoul did not speak of Prosper; and if one mentioned his name, Raoul shut his mouth and made no answer.

To the curé, of course, it was a distress and a misery. To have a hatred like this unhealed, was a blot on the parish; it was a shame, as well as a sin. At last—it was already winter, the day before Christmas—the curé made up his mind that he would put forth one more great effort.

"Look you, my son," he said to Prosper, "I am going this afternoon to Raoul Vaillantcœur to make the reconciliation. You shall give me a word to carry to him. He shall hear it this time, I promise you. Shall I tell him what you have done for him, how you have cared for him?"

"No, never," said Prosper; "you shall not take that word from me. It is nothing. It will make worse trouble. I will never send it."

"What then?" said the priest. "Shall I tell him that you forgive him?"

"No, not that," answered Prosper, "that would be a foolish word. What would that mean? It is not I who can forgive. I was the one who struck hardest. It was he that fell from the tower."

"Well, then, choose the word for yourself. What shall it be? Come, I promise you that he shall hear it. I will take with me the notary, and the good man Girard, and the little Marie Antoinette. You shall hear an answer. What message?"

"*Mon père*," said Prosper, slowly, "you shall tell him just this. I, Prosper Leclère, ask Raoul Vaillant-cœur that he will forgive me for not fighting with him on the ground when he demanded it."

Yes, the message was given in precisely those words. Marie Antoinette stood within the door, Bergeron and Girard at the foot of the bed, and the curé spoke very clearly and firmly. Vaillantcœur rolled on his pillow and turned his face away. Then he sat up in bed, grunting a little with the pain in his shoulder, which was badly set. His black eyes snapped like the eyes of a wolverine in a corner.

"Forgive?" he said, "no, never. He is a coward. I will never forgive!"

A little later in the afternoon, when the rose of sunset lay on the snowy hills, some one knocked at the door of Leclère's house.

"*Entrez!*" he cried. "Who is there? I see not very well by this light. Who is it?"

"It is me," said 'Toinette, her cheeks rosier than the snow outside, "nobody but me. I have come to ask you to tell me the rest about that new carriage —do you remember?"

III

THE voice in the canoe behind me ceased. The rain let up. The *slish, slish* of the paddle stopped. The canoe swung sideways to the breeze. I heard the *rap, rap, rap* of a pipe on the gunwale, and the quick scratch of a match on the under side of the thwart.

"What are you doing, Ferdinand?"

"I go to light the pipe, m'sieu'."

"Is the story finished?"

"But yes—but no—I know not, m'sieu'. As you will."

"But what did old Girard say when his daughter broke her engagement and married a man whose eyes were spoiled?"

"He said that Leclère could see well enough to work with him in the store."

"And what did Vaillantcœur say when he lost his girl?"

"He said it was a cursed shame that one could not fight a blind man."

"And what did 'Toinette say?"

"She said she had chosen the bravest heart in Abbéville."

"And Prosper—what did he say?"

"M'sieu', I know not. He said it only to 'Toinette."

THE GENTLE LIFE

THE GENTLE LIFE

Do you remember that fair little wood of silver birches on the West Branch of the Neversink, somewhat below the place where the Biscuit Brook runs in? There is a mossy terrace raised a couple of feet above the water of a long, still pool; and a very pleasant spot for a friendship-fire on the shingly beach below you; and a plenty of painted trilliums and yellow violets and white foam-flowers to adorn your woodland banquet, if it be spread in the month of May, when Mistress Nature is given over to embroidery.

It was there, at Contentment Corner, that Ned Mason had promised to meet me on a certain day for the noontide lunch and smoke and talk, he fishing down Biscuit Brook, and I down the West Branch, until we came together at the rendezvous. But he was late that day—good old Ned! He was occasionally behind time on a trout stream. For he went about his fishing very seriously; and if it was fine, the sport was a natural occasion of delay. But

121

if it was poor, he made it an occasion to sit down to meditate upon the cause of his failure, and tried to overcome it with many subtly reasoned changes of the fly—which is a vain thing to do, but well adapted to make one forgetful of the flight of time.

So I waited for him near an hour, and then ate my half of the sandwiches and boiled eggs, smoked a solitary pipe, and fell into a light sleep at the foot of the biggest birch tree, an old and trusty friend of mine. It seemed like a very slight sound that roused me: the snapping of a dry twig in the thicket, or a gentle splash in the water, differing in some indefinable way from the steady murmur of the stream; something it was, I knew not what, that made me aware of some one coming down the brook. I raised myself quietly on one elbow and looked up through the trees to the head of the pool. "Ned will think that I have gone down long ago," I said to myself; "I will just lie here and watch him fish through this pool, and see how he manages to spend so much time about it."

But it was not Ned's rod that I saw poking out through the bushes at the bend in the brook. It was such an affair as I had never seen before upon a trout stream: a majestic weapon at least sixteen feet long, made in two pieces, neatly spliced together in the middle, and all painted a smooth, glistening, hopeful green. The line that hung from the tip of it was also green, but of a paler, more transparent colour, quite thick and stiff where it left the rod, but tapering down towards the end, as if it were twisted of strands of horse-hair, reduced in number, until, at the hook, there were but two hairs. And the hook— there was no disguise about that—it was an unabashed bait-hook, and well baited, too. Gently the line swayed to and fro above the foaming water at the head of the pool; quietly the bait settled down in the foam and ran with the current around the edge of the deep eddy under the opposite bank; suddenly the line straightened and tautened; sharply the tip of the long green rod sprang upward, and the fisherman stepped out from the bushes to play his fish.

Where had I seen such a figure before? The dress was strange and quaint—broad, low shoes, gray woollen stockings, short brown breeches tied at the knee with ribbons, a loose brown coat belted at the waist like a Norfolk jacket; a wide, rolling collar with a bit of lace at the edge, and a soft felt hat with a shady brim. It was a costume that, with all its oddity, seemed wonderfully fit and familiar. And the face? Certainly it was the face of an old friend. Never had I seen a countenance of more quietness and kindliness and twinkling good humour.

"Well met, sir, and a pleasant day to you," cried the angler, as his eyes lighted on me. "Look you, I have hold of a good fish; I pray you put that net under him, and touch not my line, for if you do, then we break all. Well done, sir; I thank you. Now we have him safely landed. Truly this is a lovely one; the best that I have taken in these waters. See how the belly shines, here as yellow as a marsh-marigold, and there as white as a foam-flower. Is not the hand of Divine Wisdom as skilful in the colouring of a fish as in the painting of the manifold blossoms that sweeten these wild forests?"

"Indeed it is," said I, "and this is the biggest trout that I have seen caught in the upper waters of the Neversink. It is certainly eighteen inches long, and should weigh close upon two pounds and a half."

"More than that," he answered, "if I mistake not. But I observe that you call it a trout. To my mind, it seems more like a char, as do all the fish that I have caught in your stream. Look here upon these curious water-markings that run through the dark green of the back, and these enamellings of blue and gold upon the side. Note, moreover, how bright and how many are the red spots, and how each one of them is encircled with a ring of purple. Truly it is a fish of rare beauty, and of high esteem with persons of note. I would gladly know if it be as good to the taste as I have heard it reputed."

"It is even better," I replied; "as you shall find, if you will but try it."

Then a curious impulse came to me, to which I yielded with as little hesitation or misgiving, at the time, as if it were the most natural thing in the world.

"You seem a stranger in this part of the country, sir," said I; "but unless I am mistaken you are no stranger to me. Did you not use to go a-fishing in the New River, with honest Nat. and R. Roe, many years ago? And did they not call you Izaak Walton?"

His eyes smiled pleasantly at me and a little curve of merriment played around his lips. "It is a secret which I thought not to have been discovered here," he said; "but since you have lit upon it, I will not deny it."

Now how it came to pass that I was not astonished nor dismayed at this, I cannot explain. But so it was; and the only feeling of which I was conscious was a strong desire to detain this visitor as long as possible, and have some talk with him. So I grasped at the only expedient that flashed into my mind.

"Well, then, sir," I said, "you are most heartily welcome, and I trust you will not despise the only hospitality I have to offer. If you will sit down here among these birch trees in Contentment Corner, I will give you half of a fisherman's luncheon, and will cook your char for you on a board before an open wood-fire, if you are not in a hurry. Though I belong to a nation which is reported to be curious, I will promise to trouble you with no inquisitive questions; and if you will but talk to me at your will, you shall find me a ready listener."

So we made ourselves comfortable on the shady bank, and while I busied myself in splitting the fish and pinning it open on a bit of board that I had found in a pile of driftwood, and setting it up before the fire to broil, my new companion entertained me with the sweetest and friendliest talk that I had ever heard.

"To speak without offence, sir," he began, "there was a word in your discourse a moment ago that seemed strange to me. You spoke of being 'in a hurry'; and that is an expression which is unfamiliar to my ears; but if it mean the same as being in haste, then I must tell you that this is a thing which, in my judgment, honest anglers should learn to forget, and have no dealings with it. To be in haste is to be in anxiety and distress of mind; it is to mistrust Providence, and to doubt that the issue of all events is in wiser hands than ours; it is to disturb the course of nature, and put overmuch confidence in the importance of our own endeavours.

"For how much of the evil that is in the world

cometh from this plaguy habit of being in haste! The haste to get riches, the haste to climb upon some pinnacle of worldly renown, the haste to resolve mysteries—from these various kinds of haste are begotten no small part of the miseries and afflictions whereby the children of men are tormented: such as quarrels and strifes among those who would overreach one another in business; envyings and jealousies among those who would outshine one another in rich apparel and costly equipage; bloody rebellions and cruel wars among those who would obtain power over their fellow-men; cloudy disputations and bitter controversies among those who would fain leave no room for modest ignorance and lowly faith among the secrets of religion; and by all these miseries of haste the heart grows weary, and is made weak and dull, or else hard and angry, while it dwelleth in the midst of them.

"But let me tell you that an angler's occupation is a good cure for these evils, if for no other reason, because it gently dissuadeth us from haste and leadeth us away from feverish anxieties into those ways which are pleasantness and those paths which are peace. For an angler cannot force his fortune by eagerness, nor better it by discontent. He must wait upon the weather, and the height of the water, and the hunger of the fish, and many other accidents of which he has no control. If he would angle well, he must not be in haste. And if he be in haste, he will do well to unlearn it by angling, for I think there is no surer method.

"This fair tree that shadows us from the sun hath grown many years in its place without more unhappiness than the loss of its leaves in winter, which the succeeding season doth generously repair; and shall we be less contented in the place where God hath planted us? or shall there go less time to the making of a man than to the growth of a tree? This stream floweth wimpling and laughing down to the great sea which it knoweth not; yet it doth not fret because the future is hidden; and doubtless it were wise in us to accept the mysteries of life as cheerfully and go forward with a merry heart, considering that we know enough to make us happy and keep us honest for to-day. A man should be well content if he can see so far ahead of him as the next bend in the stream. What lies beyond, let him trust in the hand of God.

"But as concerning riches, wherein should you and I be happier, this pleasant afternoon of May, had we all the gold in Crœsus his coffers? Would the sun shine for us more bravely, or the flowers give forth a sweeter breath, or yonder warbling vireo, hidden in her leafy choir, send down more pure and musical descants, sweetly attuned by natural magic to woo and win our thoughts from vanity and hot desires into a harmony with the tranquil thoughts of God? And as for fame and power, trust me, sir, I have seen too many men in my time that lived very unhappily though their names were upon all lips, and died very sadly though their power was felt in many lands; too many of these great ones have I seen that spent their days in disquietude and ended them in sorrow, to make me envy their conditions or hasten to rival them. Nor do I think that, by all their perturbations and fightings and runnings to and fro, the world hath been much bettered, or even greatly changed. The colour and complexion of mortal life, in all things that are essential, remain the same under Cromwell or under Charles. The goodness and mercy of God are still over all His works, whether Presbytery or Episcopacy be set up as His interpreter. Very quietly and peacefully have I lived under several polities, civil and ecclesiastical, and under all there was room enough to do my duty and love my friends and go a-fishing. And let me tell you, sir, that in the state wherein I now find myself, though there are many things of which I may not speak to you, yet one thing is clear: if I had made haste in my mortal concerns, I should not have saved time, but lost it; for all our affairs are under one sure dominion which moveth them forward to their concordant end: wherefore '*He that believeth shall not make haste,*' and, above all, not when he goeth a-angling.

"But tell me, I pray you, is not this char cooked yet? Methinks the time is somewhat overlong for the roasting. The fragrant smell of the cookery gives me an eagerness to taste this new dish. Not that I am in haste, but—

"Well, it is done; and well done, too! Marry, the flesh of this fish is as red as rose-leaves, and as sweet as if he had fed on nothing else. The flavour of smoke from the fire is but slight, and it takes nothing from the perfection of the dish, but rather adds to it, being clean and delicate. I like not these French cooks who make all dishes in disguise, and set them forth with strange foreign savours, like a masquerade. Give me my food in its native dress, even though it be a little dry. If we had but a cup of sack, now, or a glass of good ale, and a pipeful of tobacco?

"What! you have an abundance of the fragrant weed in your pouch? Sir, I thank you very heartily! You entertain me like a prince. Not like King James, be it understood, who despised tobacco and called it a 'lively image and pattern of hell'; nor like the Czar of Russia who commanded that all who used it should have their noses cut off; but like good Queen Bess of glorious memory, who disdained not the incense of the pipe, and some say she used one herself; though for my part I think the custom of smoking one that is more fitting for men, whose frailty and need of comfort are well known, than for that fairer sex whose innocent and virgin spirits stand less in want of creature consolations.

"But come, let us not trouble our enjoyment with careful discrimination of others' scruples. Your tobacco is rarely good; I'll warrant it comes from that province of Virginia which was named for the Virgin Queen; and while we smoke together, let me call you, for this hour, my Scholar; and so I will give you four choice rules for the attainment of that unhastened quietude of mind whereof we did lately discourse.

"First: you shall learn to desire nothing in the world so much but that you can be happy without it.

"Second: you shall seek that which you desire only by such means as are fair and lawful, and this will leave you without bitterness towards men or shame before God.

"Third: you shall take pleasure in the time while you are seeking, even though you obtain not immediately that which you seek; for the purpose of a journey is not only to arrive at the goal, but also to find enjoyment by the way.

"Fourth: when you attain that which you have desired, you shall think more of the kindness of your fortune than of the greatness of your skill. This will make you grateful, and ready to share with others that which Providence hath bestowed upon you; and truly this is both reasonable and profitable, for it is but little that any of us would catch in this world were not our luck better than our deserts.

"And to these Four Rules I will add yet another —Fifth: when you smoke your pipe with a good conscience, trouble not yourself because there are men in the world who will find fault with you for so doing. If you wait for a pleasure at which no sour-complexioned soul hath ever girded, you will wait long, and go through life with a sad and anxious mind. But I think that God is best pleased with us when we give little heed to scoffers, and enjoy His gifts with thankfulness and an easy heart.

"Well, Scholar, I have almost tired myself, and, I fear, more than almost tired you. But this pipe is nearly burned out, and the few short whiffs that are left in it shall put a period to my too long discourse. Let me tell you, then, that there be some men in the world who hold not with these my opinions. They profess that a life of contention and noise and public turmoil, is far higher than a life of quiet work and meditation. And so far as they follow their own choice honestly and with a pure mind, I doubt not that it is as good for them as mine is for me, and I am well pleased that every man do enjoy his own opinion. But so far as they have spoken ill of me and my opinions, I do hold it a thing of little consequence, except that I am sorry that they have thereby embittered their own hearts.

"For this is the punishment of men who malign and revile those that differ from them in religion, or prefer another way of living; their revilings, by so much as they spend their wit and labour to make them shrewd and bitter, do draw all the sweet and wholesome sap out of their lives and turn it into poison; and so they become vessels of mockery and wrath, remembered chiefly for the evil things that they have said with cleverness.

"For be sure of this, Scholar, the more a man giveth himself to hatred in this world, the more will he find to hate. But let us rather give ourselves to charity, and if we have enemies (and what honest man hath them not?) let them be ours, since they must, but let us not be theirs, since we know better.

"There was one Franck, a trooper of Cromwell's, who wrote ill of me, saying that I neither understood the subjects whereof I discoursed nor believed the things that I said, being both silly and pretentious. It would have been a pity if it had been true. There was also one Leigh Hunt, a maker of many books, who used one day a bottle of ink whereof the gall was transfused into his blood, so that he wrote many hard words of me, setting forth selfishness and cruelty and hypocrisy as if they were qualities of my disposition. God knew, even then, whether these things were true of me; and if they were not true, it would have been a pity to have answered them; but it would have been still more a pity to be angered by them. But since that time Master Hunt and I have met each other; yes, and Master Franck, too; and we have come very happily to a better understanding.

"Trust me, Scholar, it is the part of wisdom to spend little of your time upon the things that vex and anger you, and much of your time upon the things that bring you quietness and confidence and good cheer. A friend made is better than an enemy punished. There is more of God in the peaceable beauty of this little wood-violet than in all the angry disputations of the sects. We are nearer heaven when we listen to the birds than when we quarrel with our fellow-men. I am sure that none can enter into the spirit of Christ, his evangel, save those who willingly follow his invitation when he says, '*Come ye yourselves apart into a lonely place, and rest a while.*' For since his blessed kingdom was first established in the green fields, by the lakeside, with humble fishermen for its subjects, the easiest way into it hath ever been through the wicket-gate of a lowly and grateful fellowship with nature. He that feels not the beauty and blessedness and peace of the woods and meadows that God hath bedecked with flowers for him even while he is yet a sinner, how shall he learn to enjoy the unfading bloom of the celestial country if he ever become a saint?

"No, no, sir, he that departeth out of this world without perceiving that it is fair and full of innocent sweetness hath done little honour to the every-day

137

miracles of divine beneficence; and though by mercy he may obtain an entrance to heaven, it will be a strange place to him; and though he have studied all that is written in men's books of divinity, yet because he hath left the book of Nature unturned, he will have much to learn and much to forget. Do you think that to be blind to the beauties of earth pre-pareth the heart to behold the glories of heaven? Nay, Scholar, I know that you are not of that opinion. But I can tell you another thing which perhaps you knew not. The heart that is blest with the glories of heaven ceaseth not to remember and to love the beauties of this world. And of this love I am certain, because I feel it, and glad because it is a great blessing.

"There are two sorts of seeds sown in our remembrance by what we call the hand of fortune, the fruits of which do not wither, but grow sweeter forever and ever. The first is the seed of innocent pleasures, received in gratitude and enjoyed with good companions, of which pleasures we never grow weary of thinking, because they have enriched our hearts. The second is the seed of pure and gentle sorrows, borne in submission and with faithful love, and these also we never forget, but we come to cherish them with gladness instead of grief, because we see them changed into everlasting joys. And how this may be I cannot tell you now, for you would not understand me. But that it is so, believe me: for if you believe, you shall one day see it yourself.

"But come, now, our friendly pipes are long since burned out. Hark, how sweetly the tawny thrush in yonder thicket touches her silver harp for the evening hymn! I will follow the stream downward, but do you tarry here until the friend comes for whom you were waiting. I think we shall all three meet one another, somewhere, after sunset."

I watched the gray hat and the old brown coat and long green rod disappear among the trees around the curve of the stream. Then Ned's voice sounded in my ears, and I saw him standing above me laughing.

"Hallo, old man," he said, "you're a sound sleeper! I hope you've had good luck, and pleasant dreams."

A FRIEND OF JUSTICE

A FRIEND OF JUSTICE

I

I⊤ was the black patch over his left eye that made all the trouble. In reality he was of a disposition most peaceful and propitiating, a friend of justice and fair dealing, strongly inclined to a domestic life, and capable of extreme devotion. He had a vivid sense of righteousness, it is true, and any violation of it was apt to heat his indignation to the boiling-point. When this occurred he was strong in the back, stiff in the neck, and fearless of consequences. But he was always open to friendly overtures and ready to make peace with honour.

Singularly responsive to every touch of kindness, desirous of affection, secretly hungry for caresses, he had a heart framed for love and tranquillity. But nature saw fit to put a black patch over his left eye; wherefore his days were passed in the midst of conflict and he lived the strenuous life.

How this sinister mark came to him, he never knew. Indeed it is not likely that he had any idea of the part that it played in his career. The attitude that the world took toward him from the beginning, an attitude of aggressive mistrust,—the rôle that he was expected and practically forced to assume in the drama of existence, the rôle of a hero of interminable strife,—must have seemed to him altogether mysterious and somewhat absurd. But his part was fixed by the black patch. It gave him an aspect so truculent and forbidding that all the elements of warfare gathered around him as hornets around a sugar barrel, and his appearance in public was like the raising of a flag for battle.

"You see that Pichou," said MacIntosh, the Hudson's Bay agent at Mingan, "you see yon big black-eye deevil? The savages call him Pichou because he's ugly as a lynx—'*laid comme un pichou.*' Best sledge-dog and the gurliest tyke on the North Shore. Only two years old and he can lead a team already. But, man, he's just daft for the fighting. Fought his mother when he was a pup and lamed her for life. Fought two of his brothers and nigh killed 'em both. Every dog in the place has a grudge at him, and hell's loose as oft as he takes a walk. I'm loath

"But I'll be selling him gladly."

to part with him, but I 'll be selling him gladly for fifty dollars to any man that wants a good sledge-dog, eh?—and a bit collie-shangie every week."

Pichou had heard his name, and came trotting up to the corner of the store where MacIntosh was talking with old Grant the chief factor, who was on a tour of inspection along the North Shore, and Dan Scott, the agent from Seven Islands, who had brought the chief down in his chaloupe. Pichou did not understand what his master had been saying about him: but he thought he was called, and he had a sense of duty; and besides, he was wishful to show proper courtesy to well-dressed and respectable strangers. He was a great dog, thirty inches high at the shoulder; broad-chested, with straight, sinewy legs; and covered with thick, wavy, cream-coloured hair from the tips of his short ears to the end of his bushy tail—all except the left side of his face. That was black from ear to nose—coal-black; and in the centre of this storm-cloud his eye gleamed like fire.

What did Pichou know about that ominous sign? No one had ever told him. He had no looking-glass.

He ran up to the porch where the men were sitting, as innocent as a Sunday-school scholar coming to the superintendent's desk to receive a prize. But when old Grant, who had grown pursy and nervous from long living on the fat of the land at Ottawa, saw the black patch and the gleaming eye, he anticipated evil; so he hitched one foot up on the porch, crying "Get out!" and with the other foot he planted a kick on the side of the dog's head.

Pichou's nerve-centres had not been shaken by high living. They acted with absolute precision and without a tremor. His sense of justice was automatic, and his teeth were fixed through the leg of the chief factor's boot, just below the calf.

For two minutes there was a small chaos in the post of the Honourable Hudson's Bay Company at Mingan. Grant howled bloody murder; MacIntosh swore in three languages and yelled for his dog-whip; three Indians and two French-Canadians wielded sticks and fence-pickets. But order did not arrive until Dan Scott knocked the burning embers from his big pipe on the end of the dog's nose. Pichou gasped, let go his grip, shook his head, and loped back to his quarters behind the barn, bruised, blistered, and intolerably perplexed by the mystery of life.

As he lay on the sand, licking his wounds, he remembered many strange things. First of all, there was the trouble with his mother.

She was a Labrador Husky, dirty yellowish gray, with bristling neck, sharp fangs, and green eyes, like a wolf. Her name was Babette. She had a fiendish temper, but no courage. His father was supposed to be a huge black and white Newfoundland that came over in a schooner from Miquelon. Perhaps it was from him that the black patch was inherited. And perhaps there were other things in the inheritance, too, which came from this nobler strain of blood: Pichou's unwillingness to howl with the other dogs when they made night hideous; his silent, dignified ways; his sense of fair play; his love of the water; his longing for human society and friendship.

But all this was beyond Pichou's horizon, though it was within his nature. He remembered only that Babette had taken a hate for him, almost from the first, and had always treated him worse than his all-yellow brothers. She would have starved him if she could. Once when he was half grown, she fell upon him for some small offence and tried to throttle him. The rest of the pack looked on snarling and slavering. He caught Babette by the fore-leg and broke the bone. She hobbled away, shrieking. What else could he do? Must a dog let himself be killed by his mother?

As for his brothers—was it fair that two of them should fall foul of him about the rabbit which he had tracked and caught and killed? He would have shared it with them, if they had asked him, for they ran behind him on the trail. But when they both set their teeth in his neck, there was nothing to do but to lay them both out: which he did. Afterward he was willing enough to make friends, but they bristled and cursed whenever he came near them.

It was the same with everybody. If he went out for a walk on the beach, Vigneau's dogs or Simard's dogs regarded it as an insult, and there was a fight. Men picked up sticks, or showed him the butt-end of their dog-whips, when he made friendly approaches. With the children it was different; they seemed to like him a little; but never did he follow one of them that a mother did not call from the house-door: "Pierre! Marie! come away quick! That bad dog will bite you!" Once when he ran down to the shore to watch the boat coming in from the mail-steamer, the purser had refused to let the boat go to land, and called out, "M'sieu' MacIntosh, you git no malle dis trip, eef you not call away dat dam' dog."

True, the Minganites seemed to take a certain kind of pride in his reputation. They had brought Chouart's big brown dog, Gripette, down from the Sheldrake to meet him; and after the meeting was over and Gripette had been revived with a bucket of water, everybody, except Chouart, appeared to be in good humour. The purser of the steamer had gone to the trouble of introducing a famous *boule-dogge* from Quebec, on the trip after that on which he had given such a hostile opinion of Pichou. The bull-dog's intentions were unmistakable; he expressed them the moment he touched the beach; and when they carried him back to the boat on a fish-barrow many flattering words were spoken about Pichou. He was not insensible to them. But these tributes to nis prowess were not what he really wanted. His secret desire was for tokens of affection. His position was honourable, but it was intolerably lonely and full of trouble. He sought peace and he found fights.

While he meditated dimly on these things, patiently trying to get the ashes of Dan Scott's pipe out of his nose, his heart was cast down and his spirit was disquieted within him. Was ever a decent dog so mishandled before? Kicked for nothing by a fat stranger, and then beaten by his own master!

In the dining-room of the Post, Grant was slowly and reluctantly allowing himself to be convinced that his injuries were not fatal. During this process considerable Scotch whiskey was consumed and there was much conversation about the viciousness of dogs. Grant insisted that Pichou was mad and had a devil. MacIntosh admitted the devil, but firmly denied the madness. The question was, whether the dog should be killed or not; and over this point there was like to be more bloodshed, until Dan Scott made his contribution to the argument: "If you shoot him, how can you tell whether he is mad or not? I'll give thirty dollars for him and take him home."

A FRIEND OF JUSTICE

"If you do," said Grant, "you'll sail alone, and I'll wait for the steamer. Never a step will I go in the boat with the crazy brute that bit me."

"Suit yourself," said Dan Scott. "You kicked before he bit."

At daybreak he whistled the dog down to the chaloupe, hoisted sail, and bore away for Seven Islands. There was a secret bond of sympathy between the two companions on that hundred-mile voyage in an open boat. Neither of them realized what it was, but still it was there.

Dan Scott knew what it meant to stand alone, to face a small hostile world, to have a surfeit of fighting. The station of Seven Islands was the hardest in all the district of the ancient *Postes du Roi*. The Indians were surly and crafty. They knew all the tricks of the fur-trade. They killed out of season, and understood how to make a rusty pelt look black. The former agent had accommodated himself to his customers. He had no objection to shutting one of his eyes, so long as the other could see a chance of doing a stroke of business for himself. He also had a convenient weakness in the sense of smell, when there was an old stock of pork to work off on the savages. But all of Dan Scott's senses were strong, especially his sense of justice, and he came into the Post resolved to play a straight game with both hands, toward the Indians and toward the Honourable H. B. Company. The immediate results were reproofs from Ottawa and revilings from Seven Islands. Furthermore the free traders were against him because he objected to their selling rum to the savages.

It must be confessed that Dan Scott had a way with him that looked pugnacious. He was quick in his motions and carried his shoulders well thrown back. His voice was heavy. He used short words and few of them. His eyebrows were thick and they met over his nose. Then there was a broad white scar at one corner of his mouth. His appearance was not prepossessing, but at heart he was a philanthropist and a sentimentalist. He thirsted for gratitude and affection on a just basis. He had studied for eighteen months in the medical school at Montreal, and his chief delight was to practise gratuitously among the sick and wounded of the neighbourhood. His ambi-

tion for Seven Islands was to make it a northern
suburb of Paradise, and for himself to become a
full-fledged physician. Up to this time it seemed as
if he would have to break more bones than he could
set; and the closest connection of Seven Islands appeared to be with Purgatory.

First, there had been a question of suzerainty
between Dan Scott and the local representative of
the Astor family, a big half-breed decendant of a
fur-trader, who was the virtual chief of the Indians
hunting on the Ste. Marguérite: settled by knock-
down arguments. Then there was a controversy with
Napoleon Bouchard about the right to put a fish-
house on a certain part of the beach: settled with a
stick, after Napoleon had drawn a knife. Then there
was a running warfare with Virgile and Ovide
Boulianne, the free traders, who were his rivals in
dealing with the Indians for their peltry: still un-
settled. After this fashion the record of his relations
with his fellow-citizens at Seven Islands was made
up. He had their respect, but not their affection. He
was the only Protestant, the only English-speaker,
the most intelligent man, as well as the hardest

hitter in the place, and he was very lonely. Perhaps it was this that made him take a fancy to Pichou. Their positions in the world were not unlike. He was not the first man who has wanted sympathy and found it in a dog.

Alone together, in the same boat, they made friends with each other easily. At first the remembrance of the hot pipe left a little suspicion in Pichou's mind; but this was removed by a handsome apology in the shape of a chunk of bread and a slice of meat from Dan Scott's lunch. After this they got on together finely. It was the first time in his life that Pichou had ever spent twenty-four hours away from other dogs; it was also the first time he had ever been treated like a gentleman. All that was best in him responded to the treatment. He could not have been more quiet and steady in the boat if he had been brought up to a seafaring life. When Dan Scott called him and patted him on the head, the dog looked up in the man's face as if he had found his God. And the man, looking down into the eye that was not disfigured by the black patch, saw something that he had been seeking for a long time.

All day the wind was fair and strong from the southeast. The chaloupe ran swiftly along the coast: past the broad mouth of the River Saint-Jean, with its cluster of white cottages: past the hill-encircled bay of the River Magpie, with its big fish-houses: past the fire-swept cliffs of Rivière-au-Tonnerre, and the turbulent, rocky shores of the Sheldrake: past the silver cascade of the Rivière-aux-Graines, and the mist of the hidden fall of the Rivière Manitou: past the long, desolate ridges of Cap Cormorant, where, at sunset, the wind began to droop away, and the tide was contrary. So the chaloupe felt its way cautiously toward the corner of the coast where the little Rivière-à-la-Truite comes tumbling in among the brown rocks, and found a haven for the night in the mouth of the river.

There was only one human dwelling-place in sight. As far as the eye could sweep, range after range of uninhabitable hills covered with the skeletons of dead forests; ledge after ledge of ice-worn granite thrust out like fangs into the foaming waves of the gulf. Nature, with her teeth bare and her lips scarred: this was the landscape. And in the midst of it, on a low hill above the murmuring river, surrounded by the blanched trunks of fallen trees, and the blackened débris of wood and moss, a small, square, weather-beaten palisade of rough-hewn spruce, and a patch of the bright green leaves and white flowers of the dwarf cornel lavishing their beauty on a lonely grave. This was the only habitation in sight—the last home of the Englishman, Jack Chisholm, whose story has yet to be told.

In the shelter of this hill Dan Scott cooked his supper and shared it with Pichou. When night was dark he rolled himself in his blanket, and slept in the stern of the boat, with the dog at his side. Their friendship was sealed.

The next morning the weather was squally and full of sudden anger. They crept out with difficulty through the long rollers that barred the tiny harbour, and beat their way along the coast. At Moisie they must run far out into the gulf to avoid the treacherous shoals, and to pass beyond the furious race of white-capped billows that poured from the great river for miles into the sea. Then they turned and

made for the group of half-submerged mountains
and scattered rocks that Nature, in some freak of
fury, had thrown into the throat of Seven Islands
Bay. That was a difficult passage. The black shores
were swept by headlong tides. Tusks of granite tore
the waves. Baffled and perplexed, the wind flapped
and whirled among the cliffs. Through all this the
little boat buffeted bravely on till she reached the
point of the Gran' Boule. Then a strange thing happened.

The water was lumpy; the evening was growing
thick; a swirl of the tide and a shift of the wind
caught the chaloupe and swung her suddenly around.
The mainsail jibed, and before he knew how it happened Dan Scott was overboard. He could swim
but clumsily. The water blinded him, choked him,
dragged him down. Then he felt Pichou gripping
him by the shoulder, buoying him up, swimming
mightily toward the chaloupe which hung trembling
in the wind a few yards away. At last they reached
it and the man climbed over the stern and pulled
the dog after him. Dan Scott lay in the bottom
of the boat, shivering, dazed, until he felt the dog's

cold nose and warm breath against his cheek. He flung his arm around Pichou's neck.

"They said you were mad! God, if more men were mad like you!"

II

PICHOU's work at Seven Islands was cut out for him on a generous scale. It is true that at first he had no regular canine labour to perform, for it was summer. Seven months of the year, on the North Shore, a sledge-dog's occupation is gone. He is the idlest creature in the universe.

But Pichou, being a new-comer, had to win his footing in the community; and that was no light task. With the humans it was comparatively easy. At the outset they mistrusted him on account of his looks. Virgile Boulianne asked: "Why did you buy such an ugly dog?" Ovide, who was the wit of the family, said: "I suppose M'sieu' Scott got a present for taking him."

"It's a good dog," said Dan Scott. "Treat him well and he'll treat you well. Kick him and I kick you."

Then he told what had happened off the point of Gran' Boule. The village decided to accept Pichou at his master's valuation. Moderate friendliness, with precautions, was shown toward him by everybody, except Napoleon Bouchard, whose distrust was permanent and took the form of a stick. He was a fat, fussy man; fat people seemed to have no affinity for Pichou.

But while the relations with the humans of Seven Islands were soon established on a fair footing, with the canines Pichou had a very different affair. They were not willing to accept any recommendations as to character. They judged for themselves; and they judged by appearances; and their judgment was utterly hostile to Pichou.

They decided that he was a proud dog, a fierce dog, a bad dog, a fighter. He must do one of two things: stay at home in the yard of the Honourable H. B. Company, which is a thing that no self-respecting dog would do in the summer-time, when cod-fish heads are strewn along the beach; or fight his way from one end of the village to the other, which Pichou promptly did, leaving enemies behind every fence. Huskies never forget a grudge. They are malignant to the core. Hatred is the wine of cowardly hearts. This is as true of dogs as it is of men.

Then Pichou, having settled his foreign relations, turned his attention to matters at home. There were four other dogs in Dan Scott's team. They did not want Pichou for a leader, and he knew it. They were bitter with jealousy. The black patch was loathsome to them. They treated him disrespectfully, insultingly, grossly. Affairs came to a head when Pécan, a rusty gray dog who had great ambitions and little sense, disputed Pichou's tenure of a certain hambone. Dan Scott looked on placidly while the dispute was terminated. Then he washed the blood and sand from the gashes on Pécan's shoulder, and patted Pichou on the head.

"Good dog," he said. "You're the boss."

There was no further question about Pichou's leadership of the team. But the obedience of his followers was unwilling and sullen. There was no love in it. Imagine an English captain, with a Boer company, campaigning in the Ashantee country, and you will have a fair idea of Pichou's position at Seven Islands.

He did not shrink from its responsibilities. There were certain reforms in the community which seemed to him of vital importance, and he put them through.

First of all, he made up his mind that there ought to be peace and order on the village street. In the yards of the houses that were strung along it there should be home rule, and every dog should deal with trespassers as he saw fit. Also on the beach, and around the fish-shanties, and under the racks where the cod were drying, the right of the strong jaw should prevail, and differences of opinion should be adjusted in the old-fashioned way. But on the sandy road, bordered with a broken board-walk, which ran between the houses and the beach, courtesy and propriety must be observed. Visitors walked there. Children played there. It was the general promenade. It must be kept peaceful and decent. This was the First Law of the Dogs of Seven Islands: If two dogs quarrel on the street they must go elsewhere to settle it. It was highly unpopular, but Pichou enforced it with his teeth.

161

The Second Law was equally unpopular: No stealing from the Honourable H. B. Company. If a man bought bacon or corned-beef or any other delicacy, and stored it an insecure place, or if he left fish on the beach over night, his dogs might act according to their inclination. Though Pichou did not understand how honest dogs could steal from their own master, he was willing to admit that this was their affair. His affair was that nobody should steal anything from the Post. It cost him many night watches, and some large battles to carry it out, but he did it. In the course of time it came to pass that the other dogs kept away from the Post altogether, to avoid temptations; and his own team spent most of their free time wandering about to escape discipline.

The Third Law was this: Strange dogs must be decently treated as long as they behave decently. This was contrary to all tradition, but Pichou insisted upon it. If a strange dog wanted to fight he should be accommodated with an antagonist of his own size. If he did not want to fight he should be politely smelled and allowed to pass through.

This Law originated on a day when a miserable,

long-legged, black cur, a cross between a greyhound and a water-spaniel, strayed into Seven Islands from heaven knows where—weary, desolate, and bedraggled. All the dogs in the place attacked the homeless beggar. There was a howling fracas on the beach; and when Pichou arrived, the trembling cur was standing up to the neck in the water, facing a semicircle of snarling, snapping bullies who dared not venture out any farther. Pichou had no fear of the water. He swam out to the stranger, paid the smelling salute as well as possible under the circumstances, encouraged the poor creature to come ashore, warned off the other dogs, and trotted by the wanderer's side for miles down the beach until they disappeared around the point. What reward Pichou got for this polite escort, I do not know. But I saw him do the gallant deed; and I suppose this was the origin of the well-known and much-resisted Law of Strangers' Rights in Seven Islands.

The most recalcitrant subjects with whom Pichou had to deal in all these matters were the team of Ovide Boulianne. There were five of them, and up to this time they had been the best team in the village.

They had one virtue: under the whip they could whirl a sledge over the snow farther and faster than a horse could trot in a day. But they had innumerable vices. Their leader, Carcajou, had a fleece like a merino ram. But under this coat of innocence he carried a heart so black that he would bite while he was wagging his tail. This smooth devil, and his four followers like unto himself, had sworn relentless hatred to Pichou, and they made his life difficult.

But his great and sufficient consolation for all toils and troubles was the friendship with his master. In the long summer evenings, when Dan Scott was making up his accounts in the store, or studying his pocket cyclopædia of medicine in the living-room of the Post, with its low beams and mysterious green-painted cupboards, Pichou would lie contentedly at his feet. In the frosty autumnal mornings, when the brant were flocking in the marshes at the head of the bay, they would go out hunting together in a skiff. And who could lie so still as Pichou when the game was approaching? Or who could spring so quickly and joyously to retrieve a wounded bird? But best of all were the long walks on Sunday afternoons, on the yellow beach that stretched away toward the Moisie, or through the fir-forest behind the Pointe des Chasseurs. Then master and dog had fellowship together in silence. To the dumb companion it was like walking with his God in the garden in the cool of the day.

When winter came, and snow fell, and waters froze, Pichou's serious duties began. The long, slim *cométique*, with its curving prow, and its runners of whalebone, was put in order. The harness of caribou-hide was repaired and strengthened. The dogs, even the most vicious of them, rejoiced at the prospect of doing the one thing that they could do best. Each one strained at his trace as if he would drag the sledge alone. Then the long tandem was straightened out, Dan Scott took his place on the low seat, cracked his whip, shouted *"Pouïtte! Pouïtte!"* and the equipage darted along the snowy track like a fifty-foot arrow.

Pichou was in the lead, and he showed his metal from the start. No need of the terrible *fouet* to lash him forward or to guide his course. A word was enough. "Hoc! Hoc! Hoc!" and he swung to the right, avoiding an air-hole. "Re-re! Re-re!" and he veered to the left, dodging a heap of broken ice. Past the mouth of the Ste. Marguérite, twelve miles; past Les Jambons, twelve miles more; past the River of Rocks and La Pentecôte, fifteen miles more; into the little hamlet of Dead Men's Point, behind the Isle of the Wise Virgin, whither the amateur doctor had been summoned by telegraph to attend a patient with a broken arm—forty-three miles for the first day's run! Not bad. Then the dogs got their food for the day, one dried fish apiece; and at noon the next day, reckless of bleeding feet, they flew back over the same track, and broke their fast at Seven Islands before eight o'clock. The ration was the same, a single fish; always the same, except when it was varied by a cube of ancient, evil-smelling, potent whale's flesh, which a dog can swallow at a single gulp. Yet the dogs of the North Shore are never so full of vigour, courage, and joy of life as when the sledges are running. It is in summer, when food is plenty and work slack, that they sicken and die.

Pichou's leadership of his team became famous. Under his discipline the other dogs developed speed

and steadiness. One day they made the distance to
the Godbout in a single journey, a wonderful run
of over eighty miles. But they loved their leader
no better, though they followed him faster. And
as for the other teams, especially Carcajou's, they
were still firm in their deadly hatred for the dog
with the black patch.

III

IT was in the second winter after Pichou's coming to
Seven Islands that the great trial of his courage
arrived. Late in February an Indian runner on snow-
shoes staggered into the village. He brought news
from the hunting-parties that were wintering far up
on the Ste. Marguérite—good news and bad. First,
they had already made a good hunting: for the
pelletrie, that is to say. They had killed many otter,
some fisher and beaver, and four silver foxes—a
marvel of fortune. But then, for the food, the chase
was bad, very bad—no caribou, no hare, no ptarmigan, nothing for many days. Provisions were very
low. There were six families together. Then *la*

grippe had taken hold of them. They were sick, starving. They would probably die, at least most of the women and children. It was a bad job.

Dan Scott had peculiar ideas of his duty toward the savages. He was not romantic, but he liked to do the square thing. Besides, he had been reading up on *la grippe*, and he had some new medicine for it, capsules from Montreal, very powerful—quinine, phenacetine, and morphine. He was as eager to try this new medicine as a boy is to fire off a new gun. He loaded the *cométique* with provisions and the medicine-chest with capsules, harnessed his team, and started up the river. Thermometer thirty degrees below zero; air like crystal; snow six feet deep on the level.

The first day's journey was slow, for the going was soft, and the track, at places, had to be broken out with snow-shoes. Camp was made at the foot of the big fall—a hole in snow, a bed of boughs, a hot fire and a blanket stretched on a couple of sticks to reflect the heat, the dogs on the other side of the fire, and Pichou close to his master.

In the morning there was the steep hill beside the fall to climb; alternately soft and slippery, now a slope of glass and now a treacherous drift of yielding feathers; it was a road set on end. But Pichou flattened his back and strained his loins and dug his toes into the snow and would not give back an inch. When the rest of the team balked the long whip slashed across their backs and recalled them to their duty. At last their leader topped the ridge, and the others struggled after him. Before them stretched the great dead-water of the river, a straight white path to No-man's-land. The snow was smooth and level, and the crust was hard enough to bear. Pichou settled down to his work at a glorious pace. He seemed to know that he must do his best, and that something important depended on the quickness of his legs. On through the glittering solitude, on through the death-like silence, sped the *cométique*, between the interminable walls of the forest, past the mouths of nameless rivers, under the shadow of grim mountains. At noon Dan Scott boiled the kettle, and ate his bread and bacon. But there was nothing for the dogs, not even for Pichou; for discipline is discipline, and the best of sledge-dogs will not run well after he has been fed.

Then forward again, along the lifeless road; slowly over rapids, where the ice was rough and broken; swiftly over still waters, where the way was level; until they came to the foot of the last lake, and camped for the night. The Indians were but a few miles away, at the head of the lake, and it would be easy to reach them in the morning.

But there was another camp on the Ste. Marguérite that night, and it was nearer to Dan Scott than the Indians were. Ovide Boulianne had followed him up the river, close on his track, which made the going easier.

"Does that *sacré bourgeois* suppose that I allow him all that *pelletrie* to himself and the *Compagnie?* Four silver fox, besides otter and beaver? *Non, merci!* I take some provision, and some whiskey. I go to make trade also." Thus spoke the shrewd Ovide, proving that commerce is no less daring, no less resolute, than philanthropy. The only difference is in the motive, and that is not always visible. Ovide camped the second night at a bend of the river, a mile below the foot of the lake. Between him and Dan Scott there was a hill covered with a dense thicket of spruce.

A FRIEND OF JUSTICE

By what magic did Carcajou know that Pichou, his old enemy, was so near him in that vast wilderness of white death? By what mysterious language did he communicate his knowledge to his companions and stir the sleeping hatred in their hearts and mature the conspiracy of revenge?

Pichou, sleeping by the fire, was awakened by the fall of a lump of snow from the branch of a shaken evergreen. That was nothing. But there were other sounds in the forest, faint, stealthy, inaudible to an ear less keen than his. He crept out of the shelter and looked into the wood. He could see shadowy forms, stealing among the trees, gliding down the hill. Five of them. Wolves, doubtless! He must guard the provisions. By this time the rest of his team were awake. Their eyes glittered. They stirred uneasily. But they did not move from the dying fire. It was no concern of theirs what their leader chose to do out of hours. In the traces they would follow him, but there was no loyalty in their hearts. Pichou stood alone by the sledge, waiting for the wolves.

But these were no wolves. They were assassins. Like a company of soldiers, they lined up together and rushed silently down the slope. Like lightning they leaped upon the solitary dog and struck him down. In an instant, before Dan Scott could throw off his blanket and seize the loaded butt of his whip, Pichou's throat and breast were torn to rags, his life-blood poured upon the snow, and his murderers were slinking away, slavering and muttering through the forest.

Dan Scott knelt beside his best friend. At a glance he saw that the injury was fatal. "Well done, Pichou!" he murmured, "you fought a good fight."

And the dog, by a brave effort, lifted the head with the black patch on it, for the last time, licked his master's hand, and then dropped back upon the snow—contented, happy, dead.

There is but one drawback to a dog's friendship. It does not last long enough.

End of the story? Well, if you care for the other people in it, you shall hear what became of them. Dan Scott went on to the head of the lake and found the Indians, and fed them and gave them his medicine, and all of them got well except two, and they continued to hunt along the Ste. Marguérite every winter and trade with the Honourable H. B. Company. Not with Dan Scott, however, for before that year was ended he resigned his post, and went to Montreal to finish his course in medicine; and now he is a respected physician in Ontario. Married; three children; useful; prosperous. But before he left Seven Islands he went up the Ste. Marguérite in the summer, by canoe, and made a grave for Pichou's bones, under a blossoming ash tree, among the ferns and wild flowers. He put a cross over it.

"Being French," said he, "I suppose he was a Catholic. But I'll swear he was a Christian."

THE WHITE BLOT

THE WHITE BLOT

I

THE real location of a city house depends upon the pictures which hang upon its walls. They are its neighbourhood and its outlook. They confer upon it that touch of life and character, that power to beget love and bind friendship, which a country house receives from its surrounding landscape, the garden that embraces it, the stream that runs near it, and the shaded paths that lead to and from its door.

By this magic of pictures my narrow, upright slice of living-space in one of the brown-stone strata on the eastward slope of Manhattan Island is transferred to an open and agreeable site. It has windows that look toward the woods and the sunset, water-gates by which a little boat is always waiting, and secret passageways leading into fair places that are frequented by persons of distinction and charm. No darkness of night obscures these outlets; no neighbour's house shuts off the view; no drifted snow of winter makes them impassable. They are always free, and through them I go out and in upon my adventures.

One of these picture-wanderings has always appeared to me so singular that I would like, if it were possible, to put it into words.

It was Pierrepont who first introduced me to the picture—Pierrepont the good-natured: of whom one of his friends said that he was like Mahomet's Bridge of Paradise, because he was so hard to cross: to which another added that there was also a resemblance in the fact that he led to a region of beautiful illusions which he never entered. He is one of those enthusiastic souls who are always discovering a new writer, a new painter, a new view from some old wharf by the river, a new place to obtain picturesque dinners at a grotesque price. He swung out of his office, with his long-legged, easy stride, and nearly ran me down, as I was plodding up-town through the languor of a late spring afternoon, on one of those duty-walks which conscience offers as a sacrifice to digestion.

"Why, what is the matter with you?" he cried,

as he linked his arm through mine, "you look outdone, tired all the way through to your backbone. Have you been reading the 'Anatomy of Melancholy,' or something by one of the new British female novelists? You will have *la grippe* in your mind if you don't look out. But I know what you need. Come with me, and I will do you good."

So saying, he drew me out of clanging Broadway into one of the side streets that run toward the placid region of Washington Square. "No, no," I answered, feeling, even in the act of resistance, the pleasure of his cheerful guidance, "you are altogether wrong. I don't need a dinner at your new-found Bulgarian *table-d'hôte*—seven courses for seventy-five cents, and the wine thrown out; nor some of those wonderful Mexican cheroots warranted to eradicate the tobacco-habit; nor a draught of your South American melon sherbet that cures all pains, except those which it causes. None of these things will help me. The doctor suggests that they do not suit my temperament. Let us go home together and have a shower-bath and a dinner of herbs, with just a reminiscence of the stalled ox—and a bout at backgammon to wind up the evening. That will be the most comfortable prescription."

"But you mistake me," said he; "I am not thinking of any creature comforts for you. I am prescribing for your mind. There is a picture that I want you to see; not a coloured photograph, nor an exercise in anatomical drawing; but a real picture that will rest the eyes of your heart. Come away with me to Morgenstern's gallery, and be healed."

As we turned into the lower end of Fifth Avenue, it seemed as if I were being gently floated along between the modest apartment-houses and old-fashioned dwellings, and prim, respectable churches, on the smooth current of Pierrepont's talk about his new-found picture. How often a man has cause to return thanks for the enthusiasms of his friends! They are the little fountains that run down from the hills to refresh the mental desert of the despondent.

"You remember Falconer," continued Pierrepont, "Temple Falconer, that modest, quiet, proud fellow who came out of the South a couple of years ago and carried off the landscape prize at the Academy last year, and then disappeared? He had no intimate friends here, and no one knew what had become of him. But now this picture appears, to show what he has been doing. It is an evening scene, a revelation of the beauty of sadness, an idea expressed in colours—or rather, a real impression of Nature that awakens an ideal feeling in the heart. It does not define everything and say nothing, like so many paintings. It tells no story, but I know it fits into one. There is not a figure in it, and yet it is alive with sentiment; it suggests thoughts which cannot be put into words. Don't you love the pictures that have that power of suggestion—quiet and strong, like Homer Martin's 'Light-house' up at the Century, with its sheltered bay heaving softly under the pallid greenish sky of evening, and the calm, steadfast glow of the lantern brightening into readiness for all the perils of night and coming storm? How much more powerful that is than all the conventional pictures of light-houses on inaccessible cliffs, with white foam streaming from them like the ends of a schoolboy's comforter in a gale of wind!

181

I tell you the real painters are the fellows who love pure nature because it is so human. They don't need to exaggerate, and they don't dare to be affected. They are not afraid of the reality, and they are not ashamed of the sentiment. They don't paint everything that they see, but they see everything that they paint. And this picture makes me sure that Falconer is one of them."

By this time we had arrived at the door of the house where Morgenstern lives and moves and makes his profits, and were admitted to the shrine of the Commercial Apollo and the Muses in Trade.

It has often seemed to me as if that little house were a silent epitome of modern art criticism, an automatic indicator, or perhaps regulator, of the æsthetic taste of New York. On the first floor, surrounded by all the newest fashions in antiquities and *bric-à-brac*, you will see the art of to-day—the works of painters who are precisely in the focus of advertisement, and whose names call out an instant round of applause in the auction-room. On the floors above, in degrees of obscurity deepening toward the attic, you will find the art of yesterday—the pictures which have passed out of the glare of popularity without yet arriving at the mellow radiance of old masters. In the basement, concealed in huge packing-cases, and marked "*Paris—Fragile*,"—you will find the art of to-morrow; the paintings of the men in regard to whose names, styles, and personal traits, the foreign correspondents and prophetic critics in the newspapers, are now diffusing in the public mind that twilight of familiarity and ignorance which precedes the sunrise of marketable fame.

The affable and sagacious Morgenstern was already well acquainted with the waywardness of Pierrepont's admiration, and with my own persistent disregard of current quotations in the valuation of works of art. He regarded us, I suppose, very much as Robin Hood would have looked upon a pair of plain yeomen who had strayed into his lair. The knights of capital, and coal barons, and rich merchants were his natural prey, but toward this poor but honest couple it would be worthy only of a Gentile robber to show anything but courteous and fair dealing.

He expressed no surprise when he heard what we wanted to see, but smiled tolerantly and led the way, not into the well-defined realm of the past, the present, or the future, but into a region of uncertain fortunes, a limbo of acknowledged but unrewarded merits, a large back room devoted to the works of American painters. Here we found Falconer's picture; and the dealer, with that instinctive tact which is the best part of his business capital, left us alone to look at it.

It showed the mouth of a little river: a secluded lagoon, where the shallow tides rose and fell with vague lassitude, following the impulse of prevailing winds more than the strong attraction of the moon. But now the unsailed harbour was quite still, in the pause of the evening; and the smooth undulations were caressed by a hundred opalescent hues, growing deeper toward the west, where the river came in. Converging lines of trees stood dark against the sky; a cleft in the woods marked the course of the stream, above which the reluctant splendours of an autumnal day were dying in ashes of roses, while three tiny clouds, poised high in air, burned red with the last glimpse of the departed sun.

On the right was a reedy point running out into the bay, and behind it, on a slight rise of ground, an antique house with tall white pillars. It was but dimly outlined in the gathering shadows; yet one could imagine its stately, formal aspect, its precise garden with beds of old-fashioned flowers and straight paths bordered with box, and a little arbour overgrown with honeysuckle. I know not by what subtlety of delicate and indescribable touches—a slight inclination in one of the pillars, a broken line which might indicate an unhinged gate, a drooping resignation in the foliage of the yellowing trees, a tone of sadness in the blending of subdued colours—the painter had suggested that the place was deserted. But the truth was unmistakable. An air of loneliness and pensive sorrow breathed from the picture; a sigh of longing and regret. It was haunted by sad, sweet memories of some untold story of human life.

In the corner Falconer had put his signature, *T. F.*, *"Larmone,"* *189–.* and on the border of the picture he had faintly traced some words, which we made out at last—

> *"A spirit haunts the year's last hours."*

Pierrepont took up the quotation and completed it—

> *"A spirit haunts the year's last hours,*
> *Dwelling amid these yellowing bowers:*
> > *To himself he talks;*
> *For at eventide, listening earnestly,*
> *At his work you may hear him sob and sigh,*
> > *In the walks;*
> *Earthward he boweth the heavy stalks*
> *Of the mouldering flowers:*
> *Heavily hangs the broad sunflower*
> > *Over its grave i' the earth so chilly;*
> *Heavily hangs the hollyhock,*
> > *Heavily hangs the tiger-lily."*

"That is very pretty poetry, gentlemen," said Morgenstern, who had come in behind us, "but is it not a little vague? You like it, but you cannot tell exactly what it means. I find the same fault in the picture from my point of view. There is nothing in it to make a paragraph about, no anecdote, no

experiment in technique. It is impossible to per‹
suade the public to admire a picture unless you can
tell them precisely the points on which they must
fix their admiration. And that is why, although the
painting is a good one, I should be willing to sell it
at a low price."

He named a sum of money in three figures, so
small that Pierrepont, who often buys pictures by
proxy, could not conceal his surprise.

"Certainly I should consider that a good bargain,
simply for investment," said he. "Falconer's name
alone ought to be worth more than that, ten years
from now. He is a rising man."

"No, Mr. Pierrepont," replied the dealer, "the
picture is worth what I ask for it, for I would not
commit the impertinence of offering a present to
you or your friend; but it is worth no more. Falconer's name will not increase in value. The cata-
logue of his works is too short for fame to take
much notice of it; and this is the last. Did you not
hear of his death last fall? I do not wonder, for it
happened at some place down on Long Island—a
name that I never saw before, and have forgotten

now. There was not even an obituary in the news-papers."

"And besides," he continued, after a pause, "I must not conceal from you that the painting has a blemish. It is not always visible, since you have failed to detect it; but it is more noticeable in some lights than in others; and, do what I will, I cannot remove it. This alone would prevent the painting from being a good investment. Its market value will never rise."

He turned the canvas sideways to the light, and the defect became apparent.

It was a dim, oblong, white blot in the middle distance; a nebulous blur in the painting, as if there had been some chemical impurity in the pigment causing it to fade, or rather as if a long drop of some acid, or perhaps a splash of salt water, had fallen upon the canvas while it was wet, and bleached it. I knew little of the possible causes of such a blot, but enough to see that it could not be erased without painting over it, perhaps not even then. And yet it seemed rather to enhance than to weaken the attraction which the picture had for me.

"Your candour does you credit, Mr. Morgenstern," said I, "but you know me well enough to be sure that what you have said will hardly discourage me. For I have never been an admirer of 'cabinet finish' in works of art. Nor have I been in the habit of buying them, as a Circassian father trains his daughters, with an eye to the market. They come into my house for my own pleasure, and when the time arrives that I can see them no longer, it will not matter much to me what price they bring in the auction-room. This landscape pleases me so thoroughly that, if you will let us take it with us this evening, I will send you a check for the amount in the morning."

So we carried off the painting in a cab; and all the way home I was in the pleasant excitement of a man who is about to make an addition to his house; while Pierrepont was conscious of the glow of virtue which comes of having done a favour to a friend and justified your own critical judgment at one stroke.

After dinner we hung the painting over the chimney-piece in the room called the study (because it was consecrated to idleness), and sat there far into the night, talking of the few times we had met Falconer at the club, and of his reticent manner, which was broken by curious flashes of impersonal confidence when he spoke not of himself but of his art. From this we drifted into memories of good comrades who had walked beside us but a few days in the path of life, and then disappeared, yet left us feeling as if we cared more for them than for the men whom we see every day; and of young geniuses who had never reached the goal; and of many other glimpses of "the light that failed," until the lamp was low and it was time to say good-night.

II

For several months I continued to advance in intimacy with my picture. It grew more familiar, more suggestive; the truth and beauty of it came home to me constantly. Yet there was something in it not quite apprehended; a sense of strangeness; a reserve which I had not yet penetrated.

One night in August I found myself practically alone, so far as human intercourse was concerned, in the populous, weary city. A couple of hours of writing had produced nothing that would bear the test of sunlight, so I anticipated judgment by tearing up the spoiled sheets of paper, and threw myself upon the couch before the empty fireplace. It was a dense, sultry night, with electricity thickening the air, and a trouble of distant thunder rolling far away on the rim of the cloudy sky—one of those nights of restless dulness, when you wait and long for something to happen, and yet feel despondently that nothing ever will happen again. I passed through a region of aimless thoughts into one of migratory and unfinished dreams, and dropped from that into an empty gulf of sleep.

How late it was when I drifted back toward the shore of consciousness, I cannot tell. But the student-lamp on the table had burned out, and the light of the gibbous moon was creeping in through the open windows. Slowly the pale illumination crept up the eastern wall, like a tide rising as the moon declined. Now it reached the mantel-shelf and overflowed the bronze heads of Homer and the Indian Bacchus and the Egyptian image of Isis with the infant Horus. Now it touched the frame of the picture and lapped over the edge. Now it rose to the shadowy house and the dim garden, in the midst of which I saw the white blot more distinctly than ever before.

It seemed now to have taken a new shape, like the slender form of a woman, robed in flowing white. And as I watched it through half-closed eyes, the figure appeared to move and tremble and wave to and fro, as if it were a ghost.

A haunted picture! Why should it not be so? A haunted ruin, a haunted forest, a haunted ship,—all these have been seen, or imagined, and reported, and there are learned societies for investigating such things. Why should not a picture have a ghost in it?

My mind, in that curiously vivid state which lies between waking and sleeping, went through the form of careful reasoning over the question. If there may be some subtle connection between a house and the spirits of the people who have once lived in it, —and wise men have believed this,—why should there be any impassable gulf between a picture and the vanished lives out of which it has grown? All the human thought and feeling which have passed into it through the patient toil of art, remain forever embodied there. A picture is the most living and personal thing that a man can leave behind him. When we look at it we see what he saw, hour after hour, day after day, and we see it through his mood and impression, coloured by his emotion, tinged with his personality. Surely, if the spirits of the dead are not extinguished, but only veiled and hidden, and if it were possible by any means that their presence could flash for a moment through the veil, it would be most natural that they should come back again to hover around the work into which their experience and passion had been woven. Here, if anywhere, they would "Revisit the pale glimpses of the moon." Here, if anywhere, we might catch fleeting sight, as in a glass darkly, of the visions that passed before them while they worked.

This much of my train of reasoning along the edge of the dark, I remember sharply. But after this, all was confused and misty. The shore of consciousness receded. I floated out again on the ocean of forgotten dreams. When I woke, it was with a

quick start, as if my ship had been made fast, silently and suddenly, at the wharf of reality, and the
bell rang for me to step ashore.

But the vision of the white blot remained clear
and distinct. And the question that it had brought
to me, the chain of thoughts that had linked themselves to it, lingered through the morning, and made
me feel sure that there was an untold secret in Falconer's life and that the clew to it must be sought in
the history of his last picture.

But how to trace the connection? Every one who
had known Falconer, however slightly, was out of
town. There was no clew to follow. Even the name
"Larmone" gave me no help; for I could not find
it on any map of Long Island. It was probably the
fanciful title of some old country-place, familiar
only to the people who had lived there.

But the very remoteness of the problem, its lack
of contact with the practical world, fascinated me.
It was like something that had drifted away in the
fog, on a sea of unknown and fluctuating currents.
The only possible way to find it was to commit
yourself to the same wandering tides and drift after

It, trusting to a propitious fortune that you might be carried in the same direction; and after a long, blind, unhurrying chase, one day you might feel a faint touch, a jar, a thrill along the side of your boat, and, peering through the fog, lay your hand at last, without surprise, upon the very object of your quest.

III

As it happened, the means for such a quest were at my disposal. I was part owner of a boat which had been built for hunting and fishing cruises on the shallow waters of the Great South Bay. It was a deliberate, but not inconvenient, craft, well named the Patience; and my turn for using it had come. Black Zekiel, the captain, crew, and cook, was the very man that I would have chosen for such an expedition. He combined the indolent good-humour of the negro with the taciturnity of the Indian, and knew every shoal and channel of the tortuous waters. He asked nothing better than to set out on a voyage without a port; sailing aimlessly eastward day after

day, through the long chain of landlocked bays,
with the sea plunging behind the sand-dunes on
our right, and the shores of Long Island sleeping
on our left; anchoring every evening in some little
cove or estuary, where Zekiel could sit on the cabin
roof, smoking his corn-cob pipe, and meditating on
the vanity and comfort of life, while I pushed off
through the mellow dusk to explore every creek and
bend of the shore, in my light canoe.

There was nothing to hasten our voyage. The
three weeks' vacation was all but gone, when the
Patience groped her way through a narrow, crooked
channel in a wide salt-meadow, and entered the last
of the series of bays. A few houses straggled down
a point of land; the village of Quantock lay a little
farther back. Beyond that was a belt of woods reach-
ing to the water; and from these the south-country
road emerged to cross the upper end of the bay on
a low causeway with a narrow bridge of planks at
the central point. Here was our Ultima Thule. Not
even the Patience could thread the eye of this
needle, or float through the shallow marsh-canal
farther to the east.

196

We anchored just in front of the bridge, and as I pushed the canoe beneath it, after supper, I felt the indefinable sensation of having passed that way before. I knew beforehand what the little boat would drift into. The broad saffron light of evening fading over a still lagoon; two converging lines of pine trees running back into the sunset; a grassy point upon the right; and behind that a neglected garden, a tangled bower of honeysuckle, a straight path bordered with box, leading to a deserted house with a high, white-pillared porch—yes, it was Larmone.

In the morning I went up to the village to see if I could find trace of my artist's visit to the place. There was no difficulty in the search, for he had been there often. The people had plenty of recollections of him, but no real memory, for it seemed as if none of them had really known him.

"Queer kinder fellow," said a wrinkled old bayman with whom I walked up the sandy road; "I seen him a good deal round here, but 'twan't like havin' any 'quaintance with him. He allus kep' himself to himself, pooty much. Used ter stay round 'Squire Ladoo's place most o' the time—keepin' comp'ny with the gal I guess. Larmone? Yaas, that's what *they* called it, but we don't go much on fancy names down here. No, the painter did n' 'zactly live there, but it 'mounted to the same thing. Las' summer they was all away, house shet up, painter hangin round all the time, 's if he looked fur 'em to come back any minnit. Purfessed to be paintin', but I don see 's he did much. Lived up to Mort Halsey's; died there too; year ago this fall. Guess Mis' Halsey can tell ye most of any one 'bout him."

At the boarding-house (with wide, low verandas, now forsaken by the summer boarders), which did duty for a village inn, I found Mrs. Halsey; a notable housewife, with a strong taste for ancestry, and an uncultivated world of romance still brightening her soft brown eyes. She knew all the threads in the story that I was following; and the interest with which she spoke made it evident that she had often woven them together in the winter evenings on patterns of her own.

Judge Ledoux had come to Quantock from the South during the war, and built a house there like the one he used to live in. There were three things

he hated: slavery and war and society. But he always
loved the South more than the North, and lived like
a foreigner, polite enough, but very retired. His
wife died after a few years, and left him alone with
a little girl. Claire grew up as pretty as a picture,
but very shy and delicate. About two years ago Mr.
Falconer had come down from the city; he stayed at
Larmone first, and then he came to the boarding-
house, but he was over at the Ledoux' house almost
all the time. He was a Southerner too, and a rela-
tive of the family; a real gentleman, and very proud
though he was poor. It seemed strange that he
should not live with them, but perhaps he felt more
free over here. Every one thought he must be en-
gaged to Claire, but he was not the kind of a man
that you could ask questions about himself. A year
ago last winter he had gone up to the city and
taken all his things with him. He had never stayed
away so long before. In the spring the Ledoux had
gone to Europe; Claire seemed to be falling into a
decline; her sight seemed to be failing, and her
father said she must see a famous doctor and have
a change of air.

"Mr. Falconer came back in May," continued the good lady, "as if he expected to find them. But the house was shut up and nobody knew just where they were. He seemed to be all taken aback; it was queer if he didn't know about it, intimate as he had been; but he never said anything, and made no inquiries; just seemed to be waiting, as if there was nothing else for him to do. We would have told him in a minute, if we had anything to tell. But all we could do was to guess there must have been some kind of a quarrel between him and the Judge; and if there was, he must know best about it himself.

"All summer long he kept going over to the house and wandering around in the garden. In the fall he began to paint a picture, but it was very slow painting; he would go over in the afternoon and come back long after dark, damp with the dew and fog. He kept growing paler and weaker and more silent. Some days he did not speak more than a dozen words, but always kind and pleasant. He was just dwindling away; and when the picture was almost done a fever took hold of him. The doctor said it was malaria, but it seemed to me more like a trouble in the throat, a kind of dumb misery. And one night, in the third quarter of the moon, just after the tide turned to run out, he raised up in the bed and tried to speak, but he was gone.

"We tried to find out his relations, but there didn't seem to be any, except the Ledoux, and they were out of reach. So we sent the picture up to our cousin in Brooklyn, and it sold for about enough to pay Mr. Falconer's summer's board and the cost of his funeral. There was nothing else that he left of any value, except a few books; perhaps you would like to look at them, if you were his friend?

"I never saw any one that I seemed to know so little and like so well. It was a disappointment in love, of course, and they all said that he died of a broken heart, but I think it was because his heart was too full, and wouldn't break.

"And oh!—I forgot to tell you; a week after he was gone there was a notice in the paper that Claire Ledoux had died suddenly, on the last of August, at some place in Switzerland. Her father is still away travelling. And so the whole story is broken off and will never be finished. Will you look at the books?"

Nothing is more pathetic, to my mind, than to take up the books of one who is dead. Here is his name, with perhaps a note of the place where the volume was bought or read, and the marks on the pages that he liked best. Here are the passages that gave him pleasure, and the thoughts that entered into his life and formed it; they became part of him, but where has he carried them now?

Falconer's little library was an unstudied choice, and gave a hint of his character. There was a New Testament in French, with his name written in a slender, woman's hand; three or four volumes of stories, Cable's "Old Creole Days," Allen's "Kentucky Cardinal," Page's "In Old Virginia," and the like; "Henry Esmond" and Amiel's "Journal" and Lamartine's "Raphael"; and a few volumes of poetry, among them one of Sidney Lanier's, and one of Tennyson's earlier poems.

There was also a little morocco-bound book of manuscript notes. This I begged permission to carry away with me, hoping to find in it something which would throw light upon my picture, perhaps even some message to be carried, some hint or suggestion of something which the writer would fain have had done for him, and which I promised myself faithfully to perform, as a test of an imagined friendship—imagined not in the future, but in the impossible past.

I read the book in this spirit, searching its pages carefully, through the long afternoon, in the solitary cabin of my boat. There was nothing at first but an ordinary diary; a record of the work and self-denials of a poor student of art. Then came the date of his first visit to Larmone, and an expression of the pleasure of being with his own people again after a lonely life, and some chronicle of his occupations there, studies for pictures, and idle days that were summed up in a phrase: "On the bay," or "In the woods."

After this the regular succession of dates was broken, and there followed a few scraps of verse, irregular and unfinished, bound together by the thread of a name—"Claire among her Roses," "A Ride through the Pines with Claire," "An Old Song of Claire's," "The Blue Flower in Claire's Eyes." It was not poetry, but such an unconscious tribute to the power and beauty of poetry as unfolds itself almost inevitably from youthful love, as naturally as the blossoms unfold from the apple trees in May. If you pick them they are worthless. They charm only in their own time and place.

A date told of his change from Larmone to the village, and this was written below it: "Too heavy a sense of obligation destroys freedom, and only a free man can dare to love."

Then came a number of fragments indicating trouble of mind and hesitation; the sensitiveness of the artist, the delicate, self-tormenting scruples of the lonely idealist, the morbid pride of the young poor man, contending with an impetuous passion and forcing it to surrender, or at least to compromise.

"What right has a man to demand everything and offer nothing in return except an ambition and a hope? Love must come as a giver, not as a beggar."

"A knight should not ask to wear his lady's colours until he has won his spurs."

"King Cophetua and the beggar-maid—very fine! but the other way—humiliating!"

"A woman may take everything from a man, wealth and fame and position. But there is only one thing that a man may accept from a woman—something that she alone can give—happiness."

"Self-respect is less than love, but it is the trellis that holds love up from the ground; break it down, and all the flowers are in the dust, the fruit is spoiled."

"And yet"—so the man's thought shone through everywhere—"I think she must know that I love her, and why I cannot speak."

One entry was written in a clearer, stronger hand: "An end of hesitation. The longest way is the shortest. I am going to the city to work for the Academy prize, to think of nothing else until I win it, and then come back with it to Claire, to tell her that I have a future, and that it is hers. If I spoke of it now it would be like claiming the reward before I had done the work. I have told her only that I am going to prove myself an artist, *and to live for what I love best*. She understood, I am sure, for she would not lift her eyes to me, but her hand trembled as she gave me the blue flower from her belt."

The date of his return to Larmone was marked, but the page was blank, as the day had been.

Some pages of dull self-reproach and questioning and bewildered regret followed.

"Is it possible that she has gone away, without a word, without a sign, after what has passed between us? It is not fair. Surely I had some claim."

"But what claim, after all? I asked for nothing. And was it not pride that kept me silent, taking it for granted that if I asked, she would give?"

"It was a mistake; she did not understand, nor care."

"It was my fault; I might at least have told her that I loved her, though she could not have answered me."

"It is too late now. To-night, while I was finishing the picture, I saw her in the garden. Her spirit, all in white, with a blue flower in her belt. I knew she was dead across the sea. I tried to call to her, but my voice made no sound. She seemed not to see me. She moved like one in a dream, straight on, and vanished. Is there no one who can tell her? Must she never know that I loved her?"

THE WHITE BLOT

The last thing in the book was a printed scrap of paper that lay between the leaves:

IRREVOCABLE

" Would the gods might give
Another field for human strife;
Man must live one life
Ere he learns to live.
Ah, friend, in thy deep grave,
What now can change; what now can save?"

So there was a message after all, but it could never be carried; a task for a friend, but it was impossible. What better thing could I do with the poor little book than bury it in the garden in the shadow of Larmone? The story of a silent fault, hidden in silence. How many of life's deepest tragedies are only that: no great transgression, no shock of conflict, no sudden catastrophe with its answering thrill of courage and resistance: only a mistake made in the darkness, and under the guidance of what seemed a true and noble motive; a failure to see the right path at the right moment, and a long wandering beyond it; a word left unspoken until the ears

that should have heard it are sealed, and the tongue
that should have spoken it is dumb.

The soft sea-fog clothed the night with clinging
darkness; the faded leaves hung slack and motionless from the trees, waiting for their fall; the tense
notes of the surf beyond the sand-dunes vibrated
through the damp air like chords from some mighty
violono; large, warm drops wept from the arbour
while I sat in the garden, holding the poor little
book, and thinking of the white blot in the record
of a life that was too proud to bend to the happiness that was meant for it.

There are men like that: not many perhaps, but a
few; and they are the ones who suffer most keenly
in this world of half-understanding and clouded
knowledge. There is a pride, honourable and sensitive, that imperils the realization of love, puts it
under a spell of silence and reserve, makes it sterile
of blossoms and impotent of fruits. For what is it,
after all, but a subtle, spiritual worship of self? And
what was Falconer's resolve not to tell this girl that
he loved her until he had won fame and position,
but a secret, unconscious setting of himself above

her? For surely, if love is supreme, it does not need to wait for anything else to lend it worth and dignity. The very sweetness and power of it lie in the confession of one life as dependent upon another for its fulfilment. It is made strong in its very weakness. It is the only thing, after all, that can break the prison bars and set the heart free from itself. The pride that hinders it, enslaves it. Love's first duty is to be true to itself, in word and deed. Then, having spoken truth and acted verity, it may call on honour to keep it pure and steadfast.

If Falconer had trusted Claire, and showed her his heart without reserve, would she not have understood him and helped him? It was the pride of independence, the passion of self-reliance that drew him away from her and divided his heart from hers in a dumb isolation. But Claire,—was not she also in fault? Might she not have known, should not she have taken for granted, the truth which must have been so easy to read in Falconer's face, though he never put it into words? And yet with her there was something very different from the pride that kept him silent. The virgin reserve of a young girl's heart is more sacred than any pride of self. It is the maiden instinct which makes the woman always the shrine, and never the pilgrim. She is not the seeker, but the one sought. She dares not take anything for granted. She has the right to wait for the voice, the word, the avowal. Then, and not till then, if the pilgrim be the chosen one, the shrine may open to receive him.

Not all women believe this; but those who do are the ones best worth seeking and winning. And Claire was one of them. It seemed to me, as I mused, half dreaming, on the unfinished story of these two lives that had missed each other in the darkness, that I could see her figure moving through the garden, beyond where the pallid bloom of the tall cosmos-flower bent to the fitful breeze. Her robe was like the waving of the mist. Her face was fair, and very fair, for all its sadness: a blue flower, faint as a shadow on the snow, trembled at her waist, as she paced to and fro along the path.

I murmured to myself, "Yet he loved her: and she loved him. Can pride be stronger than love?"

Perhaps, after all, the lingering and belated confession which Falconer had written in his diary might in some way come to her. Perhaps if it were left here in the bower of honeysuckles where they had so often sat together, it might be a sign and omen of the meeting of these two souls that had lost each other in the dark of the world. Perhaps,—ah, who can tell that it is not so?—for those who truly love, with all their errors, with all their faults, there is no "irrevocable"—there is "another field."

As I turned from the garden, the tense note of the surf vibrated through the night. The pattering drops of dew rustled as they fell from the leaves of the honeysuckle. But underneath these sounds it seemed as if I heard a deep voice saying "Claire!" and a woman's lips whispering "Temple!"

A YEAR OF NOBILITY

A YEAR OF NOBILITY

I

ENTER THE MARQUIS

THE Marquis sat by the camp-fire peeling potatoes.

To look at him, you never would have taken him for a marquis. His costume was a pair of corduroy trousers; a blue flannel shirt, patched at elbows with gray; lumberman's boots, flat-footed, shapeless, with loose leather legs strapped just below the knee, and wrinkled like the hide of an ancient rhinoceros; and a soft brown hat with several holes in the crown, as if it had done duty, at some time in its history, as an impromptu target in a shooting-match. A red woollen scarf twisted about his loins gave a touch of colour and picturesqueness.

It was not exactly a court dress, but it sat well on the powerful sinewy figure of the man. He never gave a thought to his looks, but peeled his potatoes with a dexterity which betrayed a past-master of the humble art, and threw the skins into the fire.

215

"Look you, m'sieu'," he said to young Winthrop Alden, who sat on a fallen tree near him, mending the fly-rod which he had broken in the morning's fishing, "look you, it is an affair of the most strange, yet of the most certain. We have known always that ours was a good family. The name tells it. The Lamottes are of *la haute classe* in France. But here, in Canada, we are poor. Yet the good blood dies not with the poverty. It is buried, hidden, but it remains the same. It is like these *pataques*. You plant good ones for seed: you get a good crop. You plant bad ones: you get a bad crop. But we did not know about the title in our family. No. We thought ours was a side-branch, an off-shoot. It was a great surprise to us. But it is certain,—beyond a doubt."

Jean Lamotte's deep voice was quiet and steady. It had the tone of assured conviction. His bright blue eyes above his ruddy mustache and bronzed cheeks, were clear and tranquil as those of a child.

Alden was immensely interested and amused. He was a member of the Boston branch of the Society for Ancestral Culture, and he recognized the favourite tenet of his sect,—the doctrine that "blood will tell." He was also a Harvard man, knowing almost everything and believing hardly anything. Heredity was one of the few unquestioned articles of his creed. But the form in which this familiar confession of faith came to him, on the banks of the Grande Décharge, from the lips of a somewhat ragged and distinctly illiterate Canadian guide, was grotesque enough to satisfy the most modern taste for new sensations. He listened with an air of gravity, and a delighted sense of the humour of the situation.

"How did you find it out?" he asked.

"Well, then," continued Jean, "I will tell you how the news came to me. It was at St. Gédéon, one Sunday last March. The snow was good and hard, and I drove in, ten miles on the lake, from our house opposite Grosse Île. After mass, a man, evidently of the city, comes to me in the stable while I feed the horse, and salutes me.

"'Is this Jean Lamotte?'

"'At your service, m'sieu'.'

"'Son of François Louis Lamotte?'

"'Of no other. But he is dead, God give him repose.'

"'I been looking for you all through Charlevoix and Chicoutimi.'

"'Here you find me then, and good-day to you,' says I, a little short, for I was beginning to be shy of him.

"'Chut, chut,' says he, very friendly. 'I suppose you have time to talk a bit. How would you like to be a marquis and have a castle in France with a hundred thousand dollars?'

"For a moment I think I will lick him; then I laugh. 'Very well indeed,' says I, 'and also a handful of stars for buckshot, and the new moon for a canoe.'

"'But no,' answers the man. 'I am earnest, Monsieur Lamotte. I want to talk a long talk with you. Do you permit that I accompany you to your residence?'

"Residence! You know that little farm-house of logs where my mother lives,—you saw it last summer. But of course it is a pretty good house. It is clean. It is warm. So I bring the man home in the sleigh. All that evening he tells the story. How our name Lamotte is really De la Motte de la Lucière.

How there belongs to that name an estate and a title in France, now thirty years with no one to claim it. How he, being an *avocat*, has remarked the likeness of the names. How he has tracked the family through Montmorency and Quebec, in all the parish-books. How he finds my great-grandfather's great-grandfather, Etienne de La Motte who came to Canada two hundred years ago, a younger son of the Marquis de la Lucière. How he has the papers, many of them, with red seals on them. I saw them. 'Of course,' says he, 'there are others of the family here to share the property. It must be divided. But it is large—enormous—millions of francs. And the largest share is yours, and the title, and a castle—a castle larger than Price's saw-mill at Chicoutimi; with carpets, and electric lights, and coloured pictures on the wall, like the hotel at Roberval.'

"When my mother heard about that she was pleased. But me—when I heard that I was a marquis, I knew it was true."

Jean's blue eyes were wide open now, and sparkling brightly. He had put down the pan of potatoes. He was holding his head up and talking eagerly.

Alden turned away his face to light his pipe, and hide a smile. "Did he get—any money—out of you?"—came slowly between the puffs of smoke.

"Money!" answered Jean, "of course there must be money to carry on an affair of this kind. There was seventy dollars that I had cleaned up on the lumber-job last winter, and the mother had forty dollars from the cow she sold in the fall. A hundred and ten dollars,—we gave him that. He has gone to France to make the claim for us. Next spring he comes back, and I give him a hundred dollars more; when I get my property five thousand dollars more. It is little enough. A marquis must not be mean."

Alden swore softly in English, under his breath. A rustic comedy, a joke on human nature, always pleased him; but beneath his cynical varnish he had a very honest heart, and he hated cruelty and injustice. He knew what a little money meant in the backwoods; what hard and bitter toil it cost to rake it together; what sacrifices and privations must follow its loss. If the smooth prospector of unclaimed estates in France had arrived at the camp on the Grande Décharge at that moment, Alden would have introduced him to the most unhappy hour of his life.

But with Jean Lamotte it was by no means so easy to deal. Alden perceived at once that ridicule would be worse than useless. The man was far too much in earnest. A jest about a marquis with holes in his hat! Yes, Jean would laugh at that very merrily; for he was a true *voyageur*. But a jest about the reality of the marquis! That struck him as almost profane. It was a fixed idea with him. Argument could not shake it. He had seen the papers. He knew it was true. All the strength of his vigorous and healthy manhood seemed to have gone into it suddenly, as if this was the news for which he had been waiting, unconsciously, since he was born.

It was not in the least morbid, visionary, abstract. It was concrete, actual, and so far as Alden could see, wholesome. It did not make Jean despise his present life. On the contrary, it appeared to lend a zest to it, as an interesting episode in the career of a nobleman. He was not restless; he was not discontented. His whole nature was at once elated and calmed. He was not at all feverish to get away from his familiar existence, from the woods and the waters he knew so well, from the large liberty of the unpeopled forest, the joyous rush of the great river, the splendid breadth of the open sky. Unconsciously these things had gone into his blood. Dimly he felt the premonitions of homesickness for them all. But he was lifted up to remember that the blood into which these things had entered was blue blood, and that though he lived in the wilderness he really belonged to *la haute classe*. A breath of romance, a spirit of chivalry from the days when the high-spirited courtiers of Louis XIV. sought their fortune in the New World, seemed to pass into him. He spoke of it all with a kind of proud simplicity.

"It appears curious to m'sieu', no doubt, but it has been so in Canada from the beginning. There were many nobles here in the old time. Frontenac, —he was a duke or a prince. Denonville,—he was a *grand seigneur*. La Salle, Vaudreuil,—these are all noble, counts or barons. I know not the difference, but the curé has told me the names. And the old Jacques Cartier, the father of all, when he went home to France, I have heard that the King made him a lord and gave him a castle. Why not? He was a capable man, a brave man; he could sail a big ship, he could run the rapids of the great river in his canoe. He could hunt the bear, the lynx, the carcajou. I suppose all these men,—marquises and counts and barons,—I suppose they all lived hard, and slept on the ground, and used the axe and the paddle when they came to the woods. It is not the fine coat that makes the noble. It is the good blood, the adventure, the brave heart."

"Magnificent!" thought Alden. "It is the real thing, a bit of the seventeenth century lost in the forest for two hundred years. It is like finding an old rapier beside an Indian trail. I suppose the fellow may be the descendant of some gay young lieutenant of the regiment Carignan-Salières, who came out with De Tracy, or Courcelles. An amour with the daughter of a *habitant*,—a name taken at random,—who can unravel the skein? But here 's the old thread of chivalry running through all the tangles, tarnished but unbroken."

This was what he said to himself. What he said to Jean was, "Well, Jean, you and I have been to-

gether in the woods for two summers now, and marquis or no marquis, I hope this is not going to make
any difference between us."

"But certainly *not!*" answered Jean. "I am well
content with m'sieu', as I hope m'sieu' is content
with me. While I am *au bois*, I ask no better than
to be your guide. Besides, I must earn those other
hundred dollars, for the payment in the spring."

Alden tried to make him promise to give nothing
more to the lawyer until he had something sure to
show for his money. But Jean was politely non-committal on that point. It was evident that he felt
the impossibility of meanness in a marquis. Why
should he be sparing or cautious? That was for
the merchant, not for the noble. A hundred, two
hundred, three hundred dollars: What was that to
an estate and a title? Nothing risk, nothing gain!
He must live up to his rôle. Meantime he was ready
to prove that he was the best guide on the Grande
Décharge.

And so he was. There was not a man in all the
Lake St. John country who knew the woods and
waters as well as he did. Far up the great rivers

Peribonca and Misstassini he had pushed his birch canoe, exploring the network of lakes and streams along the desolate Height of Land. He knew the Grand Brulé, where the bears roam in September on the fire-scarred hills among the wide, unharvested fields of blueberries. He knew the hidden ponds and slow-creeping little rivers where the beavers build their dams, and raise their silent watercities, like Venice lost in the woods. He knew the vast barrens, covered with stiff silvery moss, where the caribou fed in the winter. On the Décharge itself, —that tumultuous flood, never failing, never freezing, by which the great lake pours all its gathered waters in foam and fury down to the deep, still gorge of the Saguenay,—there Jean was at home. There was not a curl or eddy in the wild course of the river that he did not understand. The quiet little channels by which one could drop down behind the islands while the main stream made an impassable fall; the precise height of the water at which it was safe to run the Rapide Gervais; the point of rock on the brink of the Grande Chûte where the canoe must whirl swiftly in to the shore if you did not wish to go over the cataract; the exact force of the *tourniquet* that sucked downward at one edge of the rapid, and of the *bouillon* that boiled upward at the other edge, as if the bottom of the river were heaving, and the narrow line of the *filet d'eau* along which the birch-bark might shoot in safety; the treachery of the smooth, oily curves where the brown water swept past the edge of the cliff, silent, gloomy, menacing; the hidden pathway through the foam where the canoe could run out securely and reach a favourite haunt of the ouananiche, the fish that loves the wildest water,—all these secrets were known to Jean. He read the river like a book. He loved it. He also respected it. He knew it too well to take liberties with it.

The camp, that June, was beside the Rapide des Cèdres. A great ledge stretched across the river; the water came down in three leaps, brown above, golden at the edge, white where it fell. Below, on the left bank, there was a little cove behind a high point of rocks, a curving beach of white sand, a gentle slope of ground, a tent half hidden among the birches and balsams. Down the river, the main chan-

nel narrowed and deepened. High banks hemmed it
in on the left, iron-coasted islands on the right. It
was a sullen, powerful, dangerous stream. Beyond
that, in mid-river, the Île Maligne reared its wicked
head, scarred, bristling with skeletons of dead trees.
On either side of it, the river broke away into a long
fury of rapids and falls in which no boat could
live.

It was there, on the point of the island, that the
most famous fishing in the river was found; and
there Alden was determined to cast his fly before he
went home. Ten days they had waited at the Cedars
for the water to fall enough to make the passage to
the island safe. At last Alden grew impatient. It was
a superb morning,—sky like an immense blue gen-
tian, air full of fragrance from a million bells of
pink Linnæa, sunshine flattering the great river,—a
morning when danger and death seemed incredible.

"To-day we are going to the island, Jean; the
water must be low enough now."

"Not yet, m'sieu', I am sorry, but it is not yet."

Alden laughed rather unpleasantly. "I believe you
are afraid. I thought you were a good canoeman—"

"I am that," said Jean, quietly, "and therefore,—well, it is the bad canoeman who is never afraid."

"But last September you took your *monsieur* to the island and gave him fine fishing. Why won't you do it for me? I believe you want to keep me away from this place and save it for him."

Jean's face flushed. "M'sieu' has no reason to say that of me. I beg that he will not repeat it."

Alden laughed again. He was somewhat irritated at Jean for taking the thing so seriously, for being so obstinate. On such a morning it was absurd. At least it would do no harm to make an effort to reach the island. If it proved impossible they could give it up. "All right, Jean," he said, "I'll take it back. You are only timid, that's all. François here will go down with me. We can manage the canoe together. Jean can stay at home and keep the camp. Eh, François?"

François, the second guide, was a mush of vanity and good nature, with just sense enough to obey Jean's orders, and just jealousy enough to make him jump at a chance to show his independence. He would like very well to be first man for a day,—

perhaps for the next trip, if he had good luck. He grinned and nodded his head—"All ready, m'sieu'; I guess we can do it."

But while he was holding the canoe steady for Alden to step out to his place in the bow, Jean came down and pushed him aside. "Go to bed, dam' fool," he muttered, shoved the canoe out into the river, and jumped lightly to his own place in the stern.

Alden smiled to himself and said nothing for a while. When they were a mile or two down the river he remarked, "So I see you changed your mind, Jean. Do you think better of the river now?"

"No, m'sieu', I think the same."

"Well then?"

"Because I must share the luck with you whether it is good or bad. It is no shame to have fear. The shame is not to face it. But one thing I ask of you—"

"And that is?"

"Kneel as low in the canoe as you can, paddle steady, and do not dodge when a wave comes."

Alden was half inclined to turn back, and give it

up. But pride made it difficult to say the word. Besides the fishing was sure to be superb; not a line had been wet there since last year. It was worth a little risk. The danger could not be so very great after all. How fair the river ran,—a current of living topaz between banks of emerald! What but good luck could come on such a day?

The canoe was gliding down the last smooth stretch. Alden lifted his head, as they turned the corner, and for the first time saw the passage close before him. His face went white, and he set his teeth.

The left-hand branch of the river, cleft by the rocky point of the island, dropped at once into a tumult of yellow foam and raved downward along the northern shore. The right-hand branch swerved away to the east, running with swift, silent fury. On the lower edge of this desperate race of brown billows, a huge whirlpool formed and dissolved every two or three minutes, now eddying round in a wide back-water into a rocky bay on the end of the island, now swept away by the rush of waves into the white rage of the rapids below.

There was the secret pathway. The trick was, to

dart across the right-hand current at the proper moment, catch the rim of the whirlpool as it swung backward, and let it sweep you around to the end of the island. It was easy enough at low water. But now?

The smooth waves went crowding and shouldering down the slope as if they were running to a fight. The river rose and swelled with quick, uneven passion. The whirlpool was in its place one minute; the next, it was blotted out; everything rushed madly downward—and below was hell.

Jean checked the boat for a moment, quivering in the strong current, waiting for the *tourniquet* to form again. Five seconds—ten seconds—"Now!" he cried.

The canoe shot obliquely into the stream, driven by strong, quick strokes of the paddles. It seemed almost to leap from wave to wave. All was going well. The edge of the whirlpool was near. Then came the crest of a larger wave,—slap!—into the boat. Alden shrank involuntarily from the cold water, and missed his stroke. An eddy caught the bow and shoved it out. The whirlpool receded, dissolved. The whole river rushed down upon the canoe and carried it away like a leaf.

Who says that thought is swift and clear in a moment like that? Who talks about the whole of a man's life passing before him in a flash of light? A flash of darkness! Thought is paralyzed, dumb. "What a fool!" "Good-bye!" "If—" That is about all it can say. And if the moment is prolonged, it says the same thing over again, stunned, bewildered, impotent. Then?—The rocking waves; the sinking boat; the roar of the fall; the swift overturn; the icy, blinding, strangling water—God!

Jean was flung shoreward. Instinctively he struck out, with the current and half across it, toward a point of rock. His foot touched bottom. He drew himself up and looked back. The canoe was sweeping past, bottom upward, Alden underneath it.

Jean thrust himself out into the stream again, still going with the current, but now away from shore. He gripped the canoe, flinging his arm over the stern. Then he got hold of the thwart and tried to turn it over. Too heavy! Groping underneath he caught Alden by the shoulder and pulled him out. They

The whole river rushed down upon the canoe.

would have gone down together but for the boat.

"Hold on tight," gasped Jean, "put your arm over the canoe—the other side!"

Alden, half dazed, obeyed him. The torrent carried the dancing, slippery bark past another point. Just below it, there was a little eddy.

"Now," cried Jean; "the back-water—strike for the land!"

They touched the black, gliddery rocks. They staggered out of the water; waist-deep, knee-deep, ankle-deep; falling and rising again. They crawled up on the warm moss. . . .

The first thing that Alden noticed was the line of bright red spots on the wing of a cedar-bird fluttering silently through the branches of the tree above him. He lay still and watched it, wondering that he had never before observed those brilliant sparks of colour on the little brown bird. Then he wondered what made his legs ache so. Then he saw Jean, dripping wet, sitting on a stone and looking down the river.

He got up painfully and went over to him. He put his hand on the man's shoulder.

"Jean, you saved my life—I thank you, Marquis!"

"M'sieu'," said Jean, springing up, "I beg you not to mention it. It was nothing. A narrow shave, —but *la bonne chance!* And after all, you were right,—we got to the island! But now how to get off?"

II

AN ALLIANCE OF RIVALS

YES, of course they got off—the next day. At the foot of the island, two miles below, there is a place where the water runs quieter, and a *bateau* can cross from the main shore. François was frightened when the others did not come back in the evening. He made his way around to St. Joseph d'Alma, and got a boat to come up and look for their bodies. He found them on the shore, alive and very hungry. But all that has nothing to do with the story.

Nor does it make any difference how Alden spent the rest of his summer in the woods, what kind of fishing he had, or what moved him to leave five hundred dollars with Jean when he went away.

That is all padding: leave it out. The first point of interest is what Jean did with the money. A suit of clothes, a new stove, and a set of kitchen utensils for the log house opposite Grosse Île, a trip to Quebec, a little game of "*blof Américain*" in the back room of the Hôtel du Nord,—that was the end of the money.

This is not a Sunday-school story. Jean was no saint. Even as a hero he had his weak points. But after his own fashion he was a pretty good kind of a marquis. He took his headache the next morning as a matter of course, and his empty pocket as a trick of fortune. With the nobility, he knew very well, such things often happen; but the nobility do not complain about it. They go ahead, as if it was a bagatelle.

Before the week was out Jean was on his way to a lumber-shanty on the St. Maurice River, to cook for a crew of thirty men all winter.

The cook's position in camp is curious,—half menial, half superior. It is no place for a feeble man. But a cook who is strong in the back and quick with his fists can make his office much respected. Wages, forty dollars a month; duties, to keep the pea-soup kettle always hot and the bread-pan always full, to stand the jokes of the camp up to a certain point, and after that to whip two or three of the most active humourists.

Jean performed all his duties to perfect satisfaction. Naturally most of the jokes turned upon his great expectations. With two of the principal jokers he had exchanged the usual and conclusive form of repartee,—flattened them out literally. The ordinary *badinage* he did not mind in the least; it rather pleased him.

But about the first of January a new hand came into the camp,—a big, black-haired fellow from Three Rivers, Pierre Lamotte *dit* Théophile. With him it was different. There seemed to be something serious in his jests about "the marquis." It was not fun; it was mockery; always on the edge of anger. He acted as if he would be glad to make Jean ridiculous in any way.

Finally the matter came to a head. Something happened to the soup one Sunday morning—tobacco probably. Certainly it was very bad, only fit to throw away; and the whole camp was mad. It was not really Pierre who played the trick; but it was he who sneered that the camp would be better off if the cook knew less about castles and more about cooking. Jean answered that what the camp needed was to get rid of a *badreux* who thought it was a joke to poison the soup. Pierre took this as a personal allusion and requested him to discuss the question outside. But before the discussion began he made some general remarks about the character and pretensions of Jean.

"A marquis!" said he. "This *bagoulard* gives himself out for a marquis! He is nothing of the kind,— a rank humbug. There is a title in the family, an estate in France, it is true. But it is mine. I have seen the papers. I have paid money to the lawyer. I am waiting now for him to arrange the matter. This man knows nothing about it. He is a fraud. I will fight him now and settle the matter."

If a bucket of ice-water had been thrown over Jean he could not have cooled off more suddenly. He was dazed. Another marquis? This was a complication he had never dreamed of. It overwhelmed him like an avalanche. He must have time to dig himself out of this difficulty.

"But stop," he cried; "you go too fast. This is more serious than a pot of soup. I must hear about this. Let us talk first, Pierre, and afterwards—"

The camp was delighted. It was a fine comedy,—two fools instead of one. The men pricked up their ears and clamoured for a full explanation, a debate in open court.

But that was not Jean's way. He had made no secret of his expectations, but he did not care to confide all the details of his family history to a crowd of fellows who would probably not understand and would certainly laugh. Pierre was wrong of course, but at least he was in earnest. That was something.

"This affair is between Pierre and me," said Jean. "We shall speak of it by ourselves."

In the snow-muffled forest, that afternoon, where the great tree-trunks rose like pillars of black granite from a marble floor, and the branches of spruce and fir wove a dark green roof above their heads, these two stray shoots of a noble stock tried to untangle their family history. It was little that they knew about it. They could get back to their grandfathers, but beyond that the trail was rather blind. Where they crossed neither Jean nor Pierre could tell. In fact, both of their minds had been empty vessels for the plausible lawyer to fill, and he had filled them with various and windy stuff. There were discrepancies and contradictions, denials and disputes, flashes of anger and clouds of suspicion.

But through all the voluble talk, somehow or other, the two men were drawing closer together. Pierre felt Jean's force of character, his air of natural leadership, his *bonhommie*. He thought, "It was a shame for that lawyer to trick such a fine fellow with the story that he was the heir of the family." Jean, for his part, was impressed by Pierre's simplicity and firmness of conviction. He thought, "What a mean thing for that lawyer to fool such an innocent as this into supposing himself the inheritor of the title." What never occurred to either of them was the idea that the lawyer had deceived them both. That was not to be dreamed of. To admit such a thought would have seemed to them like throwing away something of great value which they had just found. The family name, the papers, the links of the genealogy which had been so convincingly set forth, —all this had made an impression on their imagi-- nation, stronger than any logical argument. But which was the marquis? That was the question.

"Look here," said Jean at last, "of what value is it that we fight? We are cousins. You think I am wrong. I think you are wrong. But one of us must be right. Who can tell? There will certainly be something for both of us. Blood is stronger than currant juice. Let us work together and help each other. You come home with me when this job is done. The lawyer returns to St. Gédéon in the spring. He will know. We can see him together. If he has fooled you, you can do what you like to him. When—*pardon*, I mean if—I get the title, I will do the fair thing by you. You shall do the same by me. Is it a bargain?"

On this basis the compact was made. The camp was much amazed, not to say disgusted, because there was no fight. Well-meaning efforts were made at intervals through the winter to bring on a crisis.

But nothing came of it. The rival claimants had pooled their stock. They acknowledged the tie of blood, and ignored the clash of interests. Together they faced the fire of jokes and stood off the crowd; Pierre frowning and belligerent, Jean smiling and scornful. Practically, they bossed the camp. They were the only men who always shaved on Sunday morning. This was regarded as foppish.

The popular disappointment deepened into a general sense of injury. In March, when the cut of timber was finished and the logs were all hauled to the edge of the river, to lie there until the ice should break and the "drive" begin, the time arrived for the camp to close. The last night, under the inspiration drawn from sundry bottles which had been smuggled in to celebrate the occasion, a plan was concocted in the stables to humble "the nobility" with a grand display of humour. Jean was to be crowned as marquis with a bridle and blinders: Pierre was to be anointed as count, with a dipperful of harness-oil; after that the fun would be impromptu.

The impromptu part of the programme began

earlier than it was advertised. Some whisper of the plan had leaked through the chinks of the wall between the shanty and the stable. When the crowd came shambling into the cabin, snickering and nudging one another, Jean and Pierre were standing by the stove at the upper end of the long table.

"Down with the *canaille!*" shouted Jean.

"Clean out the gang!" responded Pierre.

Brandishing long-handled frying-pans, they charged down the sides of the table. The mob wavered, turned, and were lost! Helter-skelter they fled, tumbling over one another in their haste to escape. The lamp was smashed. The benches were upset. In the smoky hall a furious din arose,—as if Sir Galahad and Sir Percivale were once more hewing their way through the castle of Carteloise. Fear fell upon the multitude, and they cried aloud grievously in their dismay. The blows of the weapons echoed mightily in the darkness, and the two knights laid about them grimly and with great joy. The door was too narrow for the flight. Some of the men crept under the lowest berths; others hid beneath the table. Two, endeavouring to escape by the windows, stuck fast, exposing a broad and undefended mark to the pursuers. Here the last strokes of the conflict were delivered.

"One for the marquis!" cried Jean, bringing down his weapon with a sounding whack.

"Two for the count!" cried Pierre, making his pan crack like the blow of a beaver's tail when he dives.

Then they went out into the snowy night, and sat down together on the sill of the stable-door, and laughed until the tears ran down their cheeks.

"My faith!" said Jean. "That was like the ancient time. It is from the good wood that strong paddles are made,—eh, cousin?" And after that there was a friendship between the two men that could not have been cut with the sharpest axe in Quebec.

III

A Happy Ending which is also a Beginning

The plan of going back to St. Gédéon, to wait for the return of the lawyer, was not carried out. Several of the little gods that use their own indiscretion in arranging the pieces on the puzzle-map of life, interfered with it.

The first to meddle was that highly irresponsible deity with the bow and arrows, who has no respect for rank or age, but reserves all his attention for sex.

When the camp on the St. Maurice dissolved, Jean went down with Pierre to Three Rivers for a short visit. There was a snug house on a high bank above the river, a couple of miles from the town. A wife and an armful of children gave assurance that the race of La Motte de la Lucière should not die out on this side of the ocean.

There was also a little sister-in-law, Alma Grenou. If you had seen her you would not have wondered at what happened. Eyes like a deer, face like a mayflower, voice like the "D" string in a 'cello,—she was the picture of Drummond's girl in "The Habitant":

> "She's nicer girl on whole Comte, an' jus' got eighteen year—
> Black eye, black hair, and cheek rosee dat's lak wan Fameuse on de fall;
> But don't spik much,—not of dat kin',—I can't say she love me at all."

With her Jean plunged into love. It was not a gradual approach, like gliding down a smooth stream. It was not a swift descent, like running a lively rapid. It was a veritable plunge, like going over a *chûte*. He did not know precisely what had happened to him at first; but he knew very soon what to do about it.

The return to Lake St. John was postponed till a more convenient season: after the snow had melted and the ice had broken up—probably the lawyer would not make his visit before that. If he arrived sooner, he would come back again; he wanted his money, that was certain. Besides, what was more likely than that he should come also to see Pierre? He had promised to do so. At all events, they would wait at Three Rivers for a while.

The first week Jean told Alma that she was the prettiest girl he had ever seen. She tossed her head and expressed a conviction that he was joking. She suggested that he was in the habit of saying the same thing to every girl.

The second week he made a long stride in his wooing. He took her out sleighing on the last remnant of the snow,—very thin and bumpy,—and utilized the occasion to put his arm around her waist. She cried "*Laisse-moi tranquille, Jean!*" boxed his ears, and said she thought he must be out of his mind.

The following Saturday afternoon he craftily came behind her in the stable as she was milking the cow, and bent her head back and kissed her on the face. She began to cry, and said he had taken an unfair advantage, while her hands were busy. She hated him.

"Well, then," said he, still holding her warm shoulders, "if you hate me, I am going home to-morrow."

The sobs calmed down quickly. She bent herself forward so that he could see the rosy nape of her neck with the curling tendrils of brown hair around it.

"But," she said, "but, Jean,—do you love me for sure?"

After that the path was level, easy, and very quickly travelled. On Sunday afternoon the priest was notified that his services would be needed for a wedding, the first week in May. Pierre's consent was genial and hilarious. The marriage suited him exactly. It was a family alliance. It made everything move smooth and certain. The property would be kept together.

But the other little interfering gods had not yet been heard from. One of them, who had special charge of what remained of the soul of the dealer in unclaimed estates, put it into his head to go to Three Rivers first, instead of to St. Gédéon.

He had a good many clients in different parts of the country,—temporary clients, of course,—and it occurred to him that he might as well extract another fifty dollars from Pierre Lamotte *dit* Théophile, before going on a longer journey. On his way down from Montreal he stopped in several small towns and slept in beds of various quality.

Another of the little deities (the one that presides over unclean villages; decidedly a false god, but sufficiently powerful) arranged a surprise for the travelling lawyer. It came out at Three Rivers.

He arrived about nightfall, and slept at the hotel, feeling curiously depressed. The next morning he was worse; but he was a resolute and industrious dog, after his own fashion. So he hired a buggy and drove out through the mud to Pierre's place. They heard the wagon stop at the gate, and went out to see who it was.

The man was hardly recognizable: face pale, lips blue, eyes dull, teeth chattering.

"Get me out of this," he muttered. "I am dying. God's sake, be quick!"

They helped him to the house, and he immediately went into a convulsion. From this he passed into a raging fever. Pierre took the buggy and drove post-haste to town for a doctor.

The doctor's opinion was evidently serious, but his remarks were non-committal.

"Keep him in this room. Give him ten drops of this in water every hour. One of these powders if he becomes violent. One of you must stay with him all the time. Only one, you understand. The rest keep away. I will come back in the morning."

In the morning the doctor's face was yet more grave. He examined the patient carefully. Then he turned to Jean, who had acted as nurse.

"I thought so," said he; "you must all be vac-cinated immediately. There is still time, I hope.

But what to do with this gentleman, God knows.
We can't send him back to the town. He has the
small-pox."

That was a pretty prelude to a wedding festival.
They were all at their wit's end. While the doctor
scratched their arms, they discussed the situation,
excitedly and with desperation. Jean was the first
to stop chattering and begin to think.

"There is that old *cabane* of Poulin's up the road.
It is empty these three years. But there is a good
spring of water. One could patch the roof at one
end and put up a stove."

"Good!" said the doctor. "But some one to take
care of him? It will be a long job, and a bad one."

"I am going to do that," said Jean; "it is my
place. This gentleman cannot be left to die in the
road. *Le bon Dieu* did not send him here for that.
The head of the family"—here he stopped a moment and looked at Pierre, who was silent—"must
take the heavy end of the job, and I am ready
for it."

"Good!" said the doctor again. But Alma was
crying in the corner of the room.

Four weeks, five weeks, six weeks the vigil in the *cabane* lasted. The last patches of snow disappeared from the fields one night, as if winter had picked up its rags and vanished. The willows along the brook turned yellow; the grass greened around the spring. Scarlet buds flamed on the swamp maples. A tender mist of foliage spread over the woodlands. The choke-cherries burst into a glory of white blossoms. The bluebirds came back, fluting love-songs; and the robins, carolling ballads of joy; and the blackbirds, creaking merrily.

The priest came once and saw the sick man, but everything was going well. It was not necessary to run any extra risks. Every week after that he came and leaned on the fence, talking with Jean in the doorway. When he went away he always lifted three fingers—so—you know the sign? It is a very pleasant one, and it did Jean's heart good.

Pierre kept the *cabane* well supplied with provisions, leaving them just inside of the gate. But with the milk it was necessary to be a little careful; so the can was kept in a place by itself, under the out-of-door oven, in the shade. And beside this can Jean would find, every day, something particular,—a blossom of the red geranium that bloomed in the farmhouse window, a piece of cake with plums in it, a bunch of trailing arbutus,—once it was a little bit of blue ribbon, tied in a certain square knot—so—perhaps you know that sign too? That did Jean's heart good also.

But what kind of conversation was there in the *cabane* when the sick man's delirium had passed and he knew what had happened to him? Not much at first, for the man was too weak. After he began to get stronger, he was thinking a great deal, fighting with himself. In the end he came out pretty well—for a lawyer of his kind. Perhaps he was desirous to leave the man whom he had deceived, and who had nursed him back from death, some fragment, as much as possible, of the dream that brightened his life. Perhaps he was only anxious to save as much as he could of his own reputation. At all events, this is what he did.

He told Jean a long story, part truth, part lie, about his investigations. The estate and the title were in the family; that was certain. Jean was the probable heir, if there was any heir; that was almost sure. The part about Pierre had been a—well, a mistake. But the trouble with the whole affair was this. A law made in the days of Napoleon limited the time for which an estate could remain unclaimed. A certain number of years, and then the government took everything. That number of years had just passed. By the old law Jean was probably a marquis with a castle. By the new law?—Frankly, he could not advise a client to incur any more expense. In fact, he intended to return the amount already paid. A hundred and ten dollars, was it not? Yes, and fifty dollars for the six weeks of nursing. *Voila*, a draft on Montreal, a hundred and sixty dollars,—as good as gold! And beside that, there was the incalculable debt for this great kindness to a sick man, for which he would always be M. de la Motte's grateful debtor!

The lawyer's pock-marked face—the scars still red and angry—lit up with a curious mixed light of shrewdness and gratitude. Jean was somewhat moved. His castle was in ruins. But he remained noble—by the old law; that was something!

A few days later the doctor pronounced it safe to move the patient. He came with a carriage to fetch him. Jean, well fumigated and dressed in a new suit of clothes, walked down the road beside them to the farm-house gate. There Alma met him with both hands. His eyes embraced her. The air of June was radiant about them. The fragrance of the woods breathed itself over the broad valley. A song sparrow poured his heart out from a blossoming lilac. The world was large, and free, and very good. And between the lovers there was nothing but a little gate.

"I understand," said the doctor, smiling, as he tightened up the reins, "I understand that there is a title in your family, M. de la Motte, in effect that you are a marquis?"

"It is true," said Jean, turning his head, "at least so I think."

"So do I," said the doctor. "But you had better go in, *Monsieur le Marquis*—you keep *Madame la Marquise* waiting."

THE KEEPER OF THE LIGHT

THE KEEPER OF THE LIGHT

At long distance, looking over the blue waters of the Gulf of St. Lawrence in clear weather, you might think that you saw a lonely sea-gull, snow-white, perching motionless on a cobble of gray rock. Then, as your boat drifted in, following the languid tide and the soft southern breeze, you would perceive that the cobble of rock was a rugged hill with a few bushes and stunted trees growing in the crevices, and that the gleaming speck near the summit must be some kind of a building—if you were on the coast of Italy or Spain you would say a villa or a farm-house. Then, as you floated still farther north and drew nearer to the coast, the desolate hill would detach itself from the mainland and become a little mountain-isle, with a flock of smaller islets clustering around it as a brood of wild ducks keep close to their mother, and with deep water, nearly two miles wide, flowing between it and the shore; while the shining speck on the seaward side stood out clearly as a low, whitewashed dwelling with a sturdy round tower at one end, crowned with a big eight-sided lantern—a solitary lighthouse.

That is the Isle of the Wise Virgin. Behind it the long blue Laurentian Mountains, clothed with unbroken forest, rise in sombre ranges toward the Height of Land. In front of it the waters of the gulf heave and sparkle far away to where the dim peaks of St. Anne des Monts are traced along the southern horizon. Sheltered a little, but not completely, by the island breakwater of granite, lies the rocky beach of Dead Men's Point, where an English navy was wrecked in a night of storm a hundred years ago.

There are a score of wooden houses, a tiny, weather-beaten chapel, a Hudson Bay Company's store, a row of platforms for drying fish, and a varied assortment of boats and nets, strung along the beach now. Dead Men's Point has developed into a centre of industry, with a life, a tradition, a social character of its own. And in one of those houses, as you sit at the door in the lingering June twilight, looking out across the deep channel to where the lantern of the tower is just beginning to glow with orange radiance above the shadow of the island—in that far-away place, in that mystical hour, you should hear the story of the light and its keeper.

I

WHEN the lighthouse was built, many years ago, the island had another name. It was called the Isle of Birds. Thousands of sea-fowl nested there. The handful of people who lived on the shore robbed the nests and slaughtered the birds, with considerable profit. It was perceived in advance that the building of the lighthouse would interfere with this, and with other things. Hence it was not altogether a popular improvement. Marcel Thibault, the oldest inhabitant, was the leader of the opposition.

"That lighthouse!" said he, "what good will it be for us? We know the way in and out when it makes clear weather, by day or by night. But when the sky gets swampy, when it makes fog, then we stay with ourselves at home, or we run into La Trinité, or Pentecôte. We know the way. What? The stranger boats? *B'en!* the stranger boats need not to come

259

here, if they know not the way. The more fish, the more seals, the more everything will there be left for us. Just because of the stranger boats, to build something that makes all the birds wild and spoils the hunting—that is a fool's work. The good God made no stupid light on the Isle of Birds. He saw no necessity of it."

"Besides," continued Thibault, puffing slowly at his pipe, "besides—those stranger boats, sometimes they are lost. they come ashore. It is sad! But who gets the things that are saved, all sorts of things, good to put into our houses, good to eat, good to sell, sometimes a boat that can be patched up almost like new—who gets these things, eh? Doubtless those for whom the good God intended them. But who shall get them when this *sacré* lighthouse is built, eh? Tell me that, you Baptiste Fortin."

Fortin represented the party of progress in the little parliament of the beach. He had come down from Quebec some years ago bringing with him a wife and two little daughters, and a good many new notions about life. He had good luck at the cod-fishing, and built a house with windows at the side as well as in front. When his third girl, Nataline, was born, he went so far as to paint the house red, and put on a kitchen, and enclose a bit of ground for a yard. This marked him as a radical, an innovator. It was expected that he would defend the building of the lighthouse. And he did.

"Monsieur Thibault," he said, "you talk well, but you talk too late. It is of a past age, your talk. A new time comes to the Côte Nord. We begin to civilize ourselves. To hold back against the light would be our shame. Tell me this, Marcel Thibault, what men are they that love darkness?"

"*Torrieux!*" growled Thibault, "that is a little strong. You say my deeds are evil?"

"No, no," answered Fortin; "I say not that, my friend, but I say this lighthouse means good: good for us, and good for all who come to this coast. It will bring more trade to us. It will bring a boat with the mail, with newspapers, perhaps once, perhaps twice a month, all through the summer. It will bring us into the great world. To lose that for the sake of a few birds—*ça sera b'en de valeur!* Besides, it is impossible. The lighthouse is coming, certain."

Fortin was right, of course. But Thibault's position was not altogether unnatural, nor unfamiliar. All over the world, for the past hundred years, people have been kicking against the sharpness of the pricks that drove them forward out of the old life, the wild life, the free life, grown dear to them because it was so easy. There has been a terrible interference with bird-nesting and other things. All over the world the great Something that bridges rivers, and tunnels mountains, and fells forests, and populates deserts, and opens up the hidden corners of the earth, has been pushing steadily on; and the people who like things to remain as they are have had to give up a great deal. There was no exception made in favour of Dead Men's Point. The Isle of Birds lay in the line of progress. The lighthouse arrived.

It was a very good house for that day. The keeper's dwelling had three rooms and was solidly built. The tower was thirty feet high. The lantern held a revolving light, with a four-wick Fresnel lamp, burning sperm oil. There was one of Stevenson's new cages of dioptric prisms around the flame, and once every minute it was turned by clockwork, flashing a broad belt of radiance fifteen miles across the sea. All night long that big bright eye was opening and shutting. *"Baguette!"* said Thibault, "it winks like a one-eyed Windigo."

The Department of Marine and Fisheries sent down an expert from Quebec to keep the light in order and run it for the first summer. He took Fortin as his assistant. By the end of August he reported to headquarters that the light was all right, and that Fortin was qualified to be appointed keeper. Before October was out the certificate of appointment came back, and the expert packed his bag to go up the river.

"Now look here, Fortin," said he, "this is no fishing trip. Do you think you are up to this job?"

"I suppose," said Fortin.

"Well now, do you remember all this business about the machinery that turns the lenses? That's the main thing. The bearings must be kept well oiled, and the weight must never get out of order. The clock-face will tell you when it is running right. If anything gets hitched up here's the crank to keep it going until you can straighten the machine again.

It's easy enough to turn it. But you must never let it stop between dark and daylight. The regular turn once a minute—that's the mark of this light. If it shines steady it might as well be out. Yes, better! Any vessel coming along here in a dirty night and seeing a fixed light would take it for the Cap Loup-Marin and run ashore. This particular light has got to revolve once a minute every night from April first to December tenth, certain. Can you do it?"

"Certain," said Fortin.

"That's the way I like to hear a man talk! Now, you've got oil enough to last you through till the tenth of December, when you close the light, and to run on for a month in the spring after you open again. The ice may be late in going out and perhaps the supply-boat can't get down before the middle of April, or thereabouts. But she'll bring plenty of oil when she comes, so you'll be all right."

"All right," said Fortin.

"Well, I've said it all, I guess. You understand what you've got to do? Good-by and good luck. You're the keeper of the light now."

"Good luck," said Fortin, "I am going to keep it."

The same day he shut up the red house on the beach and moved to the white house on the island with Marie-Anne, his wife, and the three girls, Alma, aged seventeen, Azilda, aged fifteen, and Nataline, aged thirteen. He was the captain, and Marie-Anne was the mate, and the three girls were the crew. They were all as full of happy pride as if they had come into possession of a great fortune.

It was the thirty-first day of October. A snow-shower had silvered the island. The afternoon was clear and beautiful. As the sun sloped toward the rose-coloured hills of the mainland the whole family stood out in front of the lighthouse looking up at the tower.

"Regard him well, my children," said Baptiste; "God has given him to us to keep, and to keep us. Thibault says he is a Windigo. *B'en!* We shall see that he is a friendly Windigo. Every minute all the night he shall wink, just for kindness and good luck to all the world, till the daylight."

II

On the ninth of November, at three o'clock in the afternoon, Baptiste went into the tower to see that the clockwork was in order for the night. He set the dial on the machine, put a few drops of oil on the bearings of the cylinder, and started to wind up the weight.

It rose a few inches, gave a dull click, and then stopped dead. He tugged a little harder, but it would not move. Then he tried to let it down. He pushed at the lever that set the clockwork in motion.

He might as well have tried to make the island turn around by pushing at one of the little spruce trees that clung to the rock.

Then it dawned fearfully upon him that something must be wrong. Trembling with anxiety, he climbed up and peered in among the wheels.

The escapement wheel was cracked clean through, as if some one had struck it with the head of an axe, and one of the pallets of the spindle was stuck fast in the crack. He could knock it out easily enough, but when the crack came around again, the pallet would catch and the clock would stop once more. It was a fatal injury.

Baptiste turned white, then red, gripped his head in his hands, and ran down the steps, out of the door, straight toward his canoe, which was pulled up on the western side of the island.

"*Dâme!*" he cried, "who has done this? Let me catch him! If that old Thibault—"

As he leaped down the rocky slope the setting sun gleamed straight in his eyes. It was poised like a ball of fire on the very edge of the mountains. Five minutes more and it would be gone. Fifteen minutes more and darkness would close in. Then the giant's eye must begin to glow, and to wink precisely once a minute all night long. If not, what became of the keeper's word, his faith, his honour?

No matter how the injury to the clockwork was done. No matter who was to be blamed or punished for it. That could wait. The question now was whether the light would fail or not. And it must be answered within a quarter of an hour.

That red ray of the vanishing sun was like a blow

in the face to Baptiste. It stopped him short, dazed and bewildered. Then he came to himself, wheeled, and ran up the rocks faster than he had come down

"Marie-Anne! Alma!" he shouted, as he dashed past the door of the house, "all of you! To me, in the tower!"

He was up in the lantern when they came running in, full of curiosity, excited, asking twenty questions at once. Nataline climbed up the ladder and put her head through the trap-door.

"What is it?" she panted. "What has hap—"

"Go down," answered her father, "go down all at once. Wait for me. I am coming. I will explain."

The explanation was not altogether lucid and scientific. There were some bad words mixed up with it.

Baptiste was still hot with anger and the unsatisfied desire to whip somebody, he did not know whom, for something, he did not know what. But angry as he was, he was still sane enough to hold his mind hard and close to the main point. The crank must be adjusted; the machine must be ready to turn before dark. While he worked he hastily made the situation clear to his listeners.

That crank must be turned by hand, round and round all night, not too slow, not too fast. The dial on the machine must mark time with the clock on the wall. The light must flash once every minute until daybreak. He would do as much of the labour as he could, but the wife and the two older girls must help him. Nataline could go to bed.

At this Nataline's short upper lip trembled. She rubbed her eyes with the sleeve of her dress, and began to weep silently.

"What is the matter with you?" said her mother, "bad child, have you fear to sleep alone? A big girl like you!"

"No," she sobbed, "I have no fear, but I want some of the fun."

"Fun!" growled her father. "What fun? *Nom d'un chien!* She calls this fun!" He looked at her for a moment, as she stood there, half defiant, half despondent, with her red mouth quivering and her big brown eyes sparkling fire; then he burst into a hearty laugh.

"Come here, my little wild-cat," he said, drawing her to him and kissing her; "you are a good girl after all. I suppose you think this light is part yours, eh?"

The girl nodded.

"*B'en!* You shall have your share, fun and all. You shall make the tea for us and bring us something to eat. Perhaps when Alma and 'Zilda fatigue themselves they will permit a few turns of the crank to you. Are you content? Run now and boil the kettle."

It was a very long night. No matter how easily a handle turns, after a certain number of revolutions there is a stiffness about it. The stiffness is not in the handle, but in the hand that pushes it.

Round and round, evenly, steadily, minute after minute, hour after hour, shoving out, drawing in, circle after circle, no swerving, no stopping, no varying the motion, turn after turn—fifty-five, fifty-six, fifty-seven—what's the use of counting? Watch the dial; go to sleep—no! for God's sake, no sleep! But how hard it is to keep awake! How heavy the arm grows, how stiffly the muscles move, how the will creaks and groans. *Batiscan!* It is not easy for a human being to become part of a machine.

Fortin himself took the longest spell at the crank, of course. He went at his work with a rigid courage. His red-hot anger had cooled down into a shape that was like a bar of forged steel. He meant to make that light revolve if it killed him to do it. He was the captain of a company that had run into an ambuscade. He was going to fight his way through if he had to fight alone.

The wife and the two older girls followed him blindly and bravely, in the habit of sheer obedience. They did not quite understand the meaning of the task, the honour of victory, the shame of defeat. But Fortin said it must be done, and he knew best. So they took their places in turn, as he grew weary, and kept the light flashing.

And Nataline—well, there is no way of describing what Nataline did, except to say that she played the fife.

She felt the contest just as her father did, not as deeply, perhaps, but in the same spirit. She went into the fight with darkness like a little soldier. And she played the fife.

When she came up from the kitchen with the

smoking pail of tea, she rapped on the door and called out to know whether the Windigo was at home to-night.

She ran in and out of the place like a squirrel. She looked up at the light and laughed. Then she ran in and reported. "He winks," she said, "old one-eye winks beautifully. Keep him going. My turn now!"

She refused to be put off with a shorter spell than the other girls. "No," she cried, "I can do it as well as you. You think you are so much older. Well, what of that? The light is part mine; father said so. Let me turn. *Va-t-en.*"

When the first glimmer of the little day came shivering along the eastern horizon, Nataline was at the crank. The mother and the two older girls were half asleep. Baptiste stepped out to look at the sky. "Come," he cried, returning. "We can stop now, it is growing gray in the east, almost morning."

"But not yet," said Nataline; "we must wait for the first red. A few more turns. Let's finish it up with a song."

She shook her head and piped up the refrain of the old Canadian *chanson:*

"He winks," she said, "old one-eye winks beautifully."

THE KEEPER OF THE LIGHT

"En roulant ma boule-le roulant
En roulant ma bou-le."

And to that cheerful music the first night's battle was carried through to victory.

The next day Fortin spent two hours in trying to repair the clockwork. It was of no use. The broken part was indispensable and could not be replaced.

At noon he went over to the mainland to tell of the disaster, and perhaps to find out if any hostile hand was responsible for it. He found out nothing. Every one denied all knowledge of the accident. Perhaps there was a flaw in the wheel; perhaps it had broken itself. That was possible. Fortin could not deny it; but the thing that hurt him most was that he got so little sympathy. Nobody seemed to care whether the light was kept burning or not. When he told them how the machine had been turned all night by hand, they were astonished. *"Cré-ié!"* they cried, "you must have had a great misery to do that." But that he proposed to go on doing it for a month longer, until December tenth, and to begin again on April first, and go on turning the light by hand for three or four weeks more until the supply-boat came down and brought the necessary tools to repair the machine—such an idea as this went beyond their horizon.

"But you are crazy, Baptiste," they said, "you can never do it; you are not capable."

"I would be crazy," he answered, "if I did not see what I must do. That light is my charge. In all the world there is nothing else so great as that for me and for my family—you understand? For us it is the chief thing. It is my Ten Commandments. I shall keep it or be damned."

There was a silence after this remark. They were not very particular about the use of language at Dead Men's Point, but this shocked them a little. They thought that Fortin was swearing a shade too hard. In reality he was never more reverent, never more soberly in earnest.

After a while he continued, "I want some one to help me with the work on the island. We must be up all the nights now. By day we must get some sleep. I want another man or a strong boy. Is there any who will come? The Government will pay. Or if not, I will pay, *moi-même*."

There was no response. All the men hung back. The lighthouse was still unpopular, or at least it was on trial. Fortin's pluck and resolution had undoubtedly impressed them a little. But they still hesitated to commit themselves to his side.

"*B'en*," he said, "there is no one. Then we shall manage the affair *en famille. Bon soir, messieurs!*"

He walked down to the beach with his head in the air, without looking back. But before he had his canoe in the water he heard some one running down behind him. It was Thibault's youngest son, Marcel, a well-grown boy of sixteen, very much out of breath with running and shyness.

"Monsieur Fortin," he stammered, "will you—do you think—am I big enough?"

Baptiste looked him in the face for a moment. Then his eyes twinkled.

"Certain," he answered, "you are bigger than your father. But what will he say to this?"

"He says," blurted out Marcel—"well, he says that he will say nothing if I do not ask him."

So the little Marcel was enlisted in the crew on the island. For thirty nights those six people—a man, and a boy, and four women (Nataline was not going to submit to any distinctions on the score of age, you may be sure)—for a full month they turned their flashing lantern by hand from dusk to daybreak.

The fog, the frost, the hail, the snow beleaguered their tower. Hunger and cold, sleeplessness and weariness, pain and discouragement, held rendezvous in that dismal, cramped little room. Many a night Nataline's fife of fun played a feeble, wheezy note. But it played. And the crank went round. And every bit of glass in the lantern was as clear as polished crystal. And the big lamp was full of oil. And the great eye of the friendly giant winked without ceasing, through fierce storm and placid moonlight.

When the tenth of December came, the light went to sleep for the winter, and the keepers took their way across the ice to the mainland. They had won the battle, not only on the island, fighting against the elements, but also at Dead Men's Point, against public opinion. The inhabitants began to understand that the lighthouse meant something—a law, an order, a principle.

Men cannot help feeling respect for a thing when they see others willing to fight or to suffer for it.

When the time arrived to kindle the light again in the spring, Fortin could have had any one that he wanted to help him. But no; he chose the little Marcel again; the boy wanted to go, and he had earned the right. Besides, he and Nataline had struck up a close friendship on the island, cemented during the winter by various hunting excursions after hares and ptarmigan. Marcel was a skilful setter of snares. But Nataline was not content until she had won consent to borrow her father's *carabine*. They hunted in partnership. One day they had shot a fox. That is, Nataline had shot it, though Marcel had seen it first and tracked it. Now they wanted to try for a seal on the point of the island when the ice went out. It was quite essential that Marcel should go.

"Besides," said Baptiste to his wife, confidentially, "a boy costs less than a man. Why should we waste money? Marcel is best."

A peasant-hero is seldom averse to economy in small things, like money.

But there was not much play in the spring session

with the light on the island. It was a bitter job. December had been lamb-like compared with April. First, the southeast wind kept the ice driving in along the shore. Then the northwest wind came hurtling down from the Arctic wilderness like a pack of wolves. There was a snow-storm of four days and nights that made the whole world—earth and sky and sea—look like a crazy white chaos. And through it all, that weary, dogged crank must be kept turning—turning from dark to daylight.

It seemed as if the supply-boat would never come. At last they saw it, one fair afternoon, April the twenty-ninth, creeping slowly down the coast. They were just getting ready for another night's work.

Fortin ran out of the tower, took off his hat, and began to say his prayers. The wife and the two elder girls stood in the kitchen door, crossing themselves, with tears in their eyes. Marcel and Nataline were coming up from the point of the island, where they had been watching for their seal. She was singing

"Mon père n'avait fille que moi,
Encore sur la mer il m'envoi-e-eh!"

278

When she saw the boat she stopped short for a minute.

"Well," she said, "they find us awake, *n'est-c'pas?* And if they don't come faster than that we'll have another chance to show them how we make the light wink, eh?"

Then she went on with her song—

> "*Sautez, mignonne, Cécilia.*
> *Ah, ah, ah, ah, Cécilia!*"

III

You did not suppose that was the end of the story, did you?

No, an out-of-doors story does not end like that, broken off in the middle, with a bit of a song. It goes on to something definite, like a wedding or a funeral.

You have not heard, yet, how near the light came to failing, and how the keeper saved it and something else too. Nataline's story is not told; it is only begun. This first part is only the introduction, just to let you see what kind of a girl she was, and how

279

her life was made. If you want to hear the conclusion, we must hurry along a little faster or we shall never get to it.

Nataline grew up like a young birch tree—stately and strong, good to look at. She was beautiful in her place; she fitted it exactly. Her bronzed face with an under-tinge of red; her low, black eyebrows; her clear eyes like the brown waters of a woodland stream; her dark, curly hair with little tendrils always blowing loose around the pillar of her neck; her broad breast and sloping shoulders; her firm, fearless step; her voice, rich and vibrant; her straight, steady looks—but there, who can describe a thing like that? I tell you she was a girl to love out-of-doors.

There was nothing that she could not do. She could cook; she could swing an axe; she could paddle a canoe; she could fish; she could shoot; and, best of all, she could run the lighthouse. Her father's devotion to it had gone into her blood. It was the centre of her life, her law of God. There was nothing about it that she did not understand and love. From the first of April to the tenth of December the flash-

ing of that light was like the beating of her heart —
steady, even, unfaltering. She kept time to it as unconsciously as the tides follow the moon. She lived
by it and for it.

There were no more accidents to the clockwork
after the first one was repaired. It ran on regularly,
year after year.

Alma and Azilda were married and went away to
live, one on the South Shore, the other at Quebec.
Nataline was her father's right-hand man. As the
rheumatism took hold of him and lamed his shoulders and wrists, more and more of the work fell upon
her. She was proud of it.

At last it came to pass, one day in January, that
Baptiste died. He was not gathered to his fathers,
for they were buried far away beside the Montmo-
renci, and on the rocky coast of Brittany. But the
men dug through the snow behind the tiny chapel
at Dead Men's Point, and made a grave for Baptiste
Fortin, and the young priest of the mission read the
funeral service over it.

It went without saying that Nataline was to be
the keeper of the light, at least until the supply-

boat came down again in the spring and orders arrived from the Government in Quebec. Why not? She was a woman, it is true. But if a woman can do a thing as well as a man, why should she not do it? Besides, Nataline could do this particular thing much better than any man on the Point. Everybody approved of her as the heir of her father, especially young Marcel Thibault.

What?

Yes, of course. You could not help guessing it. He was Nataline's lover. They were to be married the next summer. They sat together in the best room, while the old mother was rocking to and fro and knitting beside the kitchen stove, and talked of what they were going to do. Once in a while, when Nataline grieved for her father, she would let Marcel put his arm around her and comfort her in the way that lovers know. But their talk was mainly of the future, because they were young, and of the light, because Nataline's life belonged to it.

Perhaps the Government would remember that year when it was kept going by hand for two months, and give it to her to keep as long as she lived. That would be only fair. Certainly, it was hers for the present. No one had as good a right to it. She took possession without a doubt. At all events, while she was the keeper the light should not fail.

But that winter was a bad one on the North Shore, and particularly at Dead Men's Point. It was terribly bad. The summer before, the fishing had been almost a dead failure. In June a wild storm had smashed all the salmon nets and swept most of them away. In July they could find no caplin for bait for the cod-fishing, and in August and September they could find no cod. The few bushels of potatoes that some of the inhabitants had planted, rotted in the ground. The people at the Point went into the winter short of money and very short of food.

There were some supplies at the store, pork and flour and molasses, and they could run through the year on credit and pay their debts the following summer if the fish came back. But this resource also failed them. In the last week of January the store caught fire and burned up. Nothing was saved. The only hope now was the seal-hunting in February and

March and April. That at least would bring them meat and oil enough to keep them from starvation.

But this hope failed, too. The winds blew strong from the north and west, driving the ice far out into the gulf. The chase was long and perilous. The seals were few and wild. Less than a dozen were killed in all. By the last week in March Dead Men's Point stood face to face with famine.

Then it was that old Thibault had an idea.

"There is sperm oil on the Island of Birds," said he, "in the lighthouse, plenty of it, gallons of it. It is not very good to taste, perhaps, but what of that? It will keep life in the body. The Esquimaux drink it in the north, often. We must take the oil of the lighthouse to keep us from starving until the sup-ply-boat comes down."

"But how shall we get it?" asked the others. "It is locked up. Nataline Fortin has the key. Will she give it?"

"Give it?" growled Thibault. "Nome of a name! of course she will give it. She must. Is not a life, the life of all of us, more than a light?"

A self-appointed committee of three, with Thibault at the head, waited upon Nataline without delay, told her their plan, and asked for the key. She thought it over silently for a few minutes, and then refused point-blank.

"No," she said, "I will not give the key. That oil is for the lamp. If you take it, the lamp will not be lighted on the first of April; it will not be burning when the supply-boat comes. For me, that would be shame, disgrace, worse than death. I am the keeper of the light. You shall not have the oil."

They argued with her, pleaded with her, tried to browbeat her. She was a rock. Her round under-jaw was set like a steel trap. Her lips straightened into a white line. Her eyebrows drew together, and her eyes grew black.

"No," she cried, "I tell you no, no, a thousand times no. All in this house I will share with you. But not one drop of what belongs to the light! Never!"

Later in the afternoon the priest came to see her; a thin, pale young man, bent with the hardships of his life, and with sad dreams in his sunken eyes. He talked with her very gently and kindly.

"Think well, my daughter; think seriously what you do. Is it not our first duty to save human life? Surely that must be according to the will of God. Will you refuse to obey it?"

Nataline was trembling a little now. Her brows were unlocked. The tears stood in her eyes and ran down her cheeks. She was twisting her hands together.

"My father," she answered, "I desire to do the will of God. But how shall I know it? Is it not His first command that we should love and serve Him faithfully in the duty which He has given us? He gave me this light to keep. My father kept it. He is dead. If I am unfaithful what will he say to me? Besides, the supply-boat is coming soon—I have thought of this—when it comes it will bring food. But if the light is out, the boat may be lost. That would be the punishment for my sin. No, *mon père*, we must trust God. He will keep the people. I will keep the light."

The priest looked at her long and steadily. A glow came into his face. He put his hand on her shoulder. "You shall follow your conscience," he said quietly. "Peace be with you, Nataline."

That evening just at dark Marcel came. She let him take her in his arms and kiss her. She felt like a little child, tired and weak.

"Well," he whispered, "you have done bravely, sweetheart. You were right not to give the key. That would have been a shame to you. But it is all settled now. They will have the oil without your fault. To-night they are going out to the lighthouse to break in and take what they want. You need not know. There will be no blame—"

She straightened in his arms as if an electric shock had passed through her. She sprang back, blazing with anger.

"What?" she cried, "me a thief by round-about, —with my hand behind my back and my eyes shut? Never. Do you think I care only for the blame? I tell you that is nothing. My light shall not be robbed, never, never!"

She came close to him and took him by the shoulders. Their eyes were on a level. He was a strong man, but she was the stronger then.

"Marcel Thibault," she said, "do you love me?"

"My faith," he gasped, "I do. You know I do."

"Then listen," she continued; "this is what you are going to do. You are going down to the shore at once to make ready the big canoe. I am going to get food enough to last us for the month. It will be a hard pinch, but it will do. Then we are going out to the island to-night, in less than an hour. Day after to-morrow is the first of April. Then we shall light the lantern, and it shall burn every night until the boat comes down. You hear? Now go: and be quick: and bring your gun."

IV

THEY pushed off in the black darkness, among the fragments of ice that lay along the shore. They crossed the strait in silence, and hid their canoe among the rocks on the island. They carried their stuff up to the house and locked it in the kitchen. Then they unlocked the tower, and went in, Marcel with his shot-gun, and Nataline with her father's old *carabine*. They fastened the door again, and bolted it, and sat down in the dark to wait.

Presently they heard the grating of the prow of

the barge on the stones below, the steps of men stumbling up the steep path, and voices mingled in confused talk. The glimmer of a couple of lanterns went bobbing in and out among the rocks and bushes. There was a little crowd of eight or ten men, and they came on carelessly, chattering and laughing. Three of them carried axes, and three others a heavy log of wood which they had picked up on their way.

"The log is better than the axes," said one; "take it in your hands this way, two of you on one side, another on the opposite side in the middle. Then swing it back and forwards and let it go. The door will come down, I tell you, like a sheet of paper. But wait till I give the word, then swing hard. One —two—"

"Stop!" cried Nataline, throwing open the little window. "If you dare to touch that door, I shoot."

She thrust out the barrel of the rifle, and Marcel's shot-gun appeared beside it. The old rifle was not loaded, but who knew that? Besides, both barrels of the shot-gun were full.

There was amazement in the crowd outside the tower, and consternation, and then anger.

"Marcel," they shouted, "you there? *Maudit polisson!* Come out of that. Let us in. You told us—"

"I know," answered Marcel, "but I was mistaken, that is all. I stand by Mademoiselle Fortin. What she says is right. If any man tries to break in here, we kill him. No more talk!"

The gang muttered; cursed; threatened; looked at the guns; and went off to their boat.

"It is murder that you will do," one of them called out, "you are a murderess, you Mademoiselle Fortin! you cause the people to die of hunger!"

"Not I," she answered; "that is as the good God pleases. No matter. The light shall burn."

They heard the babble of the men as they stumbled down the hill; the grinding of the boat on the rocks as they shoved off; the rattle of the oars in the rowlocks. After that the island was as still as a graveyard.

Then Nataline sat down on the floor in the dark, and put her face in her hands, and cried. Marcel tried to comfort her. She took his hand and pushed it gently away from her waist.

"No, Marcel," she said, "not now! Not that,

please, Marcel! Come into the house. I want to talk with you."

They went into the cold, dark kitchen, lit a candle and kindled a fire in the stove. Nataline busied herself with a score of things. She put away the poor little store of provisions, sent Marcel for a pail of water, made some tea, spread the table, and sat down opposite to him. For a time she kept her eyes turned away from him, while she talked about all sorts of things. Then she fell silent for a little, still not looking at him. She got up and moved about the room, arranged two or three packages on the shelves, shut the damper of the stove, glancing at Marcel's back out of the corners of her eyes. Then she came back to her chair, pushed her cup aside, rested both elbows on the table and her chin in her hands, and looked Marcel square in the face with her clear brown eyes.

"My friend," she said, "are you an honest man, *un brave garçon?*"

For an instant he could say nothing. He was so puzzled. "Why yes, Nataline," he answered, "yes, surely—I hope."

"Then let me speak to you without fear," she continued. "You do not suppose that I am ignorant of what I have done this night. I am not a baby. You are a man. I am a girl. We are shut up alone in this house for two weeks, a month, God knows how long. You know what that means, what people will say. I have risked all that a girl has most precious. I have put my good name in your hands."

Marcel tried to speak, but she stopped him.

"Let me finish. It is not easy to say. I know you are honourable. I trust you waking and sleeping. But I am a woman. There must be no love-making. We have other work to do. The light must not fail. You will not touch me, you will not embrace me—not once—till after the boat has come. Then"—she smiled at him like a sunburned angel—"well, is it a bargain?"

She put out one hand across the table. Marcel took it in both of his own. He did not kiss it. He lifted it up in front of his face.

"I swear to you, Nataline, you shall be to me as the Blessed Virgin herself."

The next day they put the light in order, and the

following night they kindled it. They still feared another attack from the mainland, and thought it needful that one of them should be on guard all the time, though the machine itself was working beautifully and needed little watching. Nataline took the night duty; it was her own choice; she loved the charge of the lamp. Marcel was on duty through the day. They were together for three or four hours in the morning and in the evening.

It was not a desperate vigil like that affair with the broken clockwork eight years before. There was no weary turning of the crank. There was just enough work to do about the house and the tower to keep them busy. The weather was fair. The worst thing was the short supply of food. But though they were hungry, they were not starving. And Nataline still played the fife. She jested, she sang, she told long fairy stories while they sat in the kitchen. Marcel admitted that it was not at all a bad arrangement.

But his thoughts turned very often to the arrival of the supply-boat. He hoped it would not be late. The ice was well broken up already and driven far out into the gulf. The boat ought to be able to run down the shore in good time.

One evening as Nataline came down from her sleep she saw Marcel coming up the rocks dragging a young seal behind him.

"Hurra!" he shouted, "here is plenty of meat. I shot it out at the end of the island, about an hour ago."

But Nataline said that they did not need the seal. There was still food enough in the larder. On shore there must be greater need. Marcel must take the seal over to the mainland that night and leave it on the beach near the priest's house. He grumbled a little, but he did it.

That was on the twenty-third of April. The clear sky held for three days longer, calm, bright, halcyon weather. On the afternoon of the twenty-seventh the clouds came down from the north, not a long furious tempest, but a brief, sharp storm, with considerable wind and a whirling, blinding fall of April snow. It was a bad night for boats at sea, confusing, bewildering, a night when the lighthouse had to do its best Nataline was in the tower all night, tending the lamp, watching the clockwork. Once it seemed to her that the lantern was so covered with snow that light could not shine through. She got her long brush and scraped the snow away. It was cold work, but she gloried in it. The bright eye of the tower, winking, winking steadily through the storm seemed to be the sign of her power in the world. It was hers. She kept it shining.

When morning came the wind was still blowing fitfully off shore, but the snow had almost ceased. Nataline stopped the clockwork, and was just climbing up into the lantern to put out the lamp, when Marcel's voice hailed her.

"Come down, Nataline, come down quick. Make haste!"

She turned and hurried out, not knowing what was to come; perhaps a message of trouble from the mainland, perhaps a new assault on the lighthouse.

As she came out of the tower, her brown eyes heavy from the night-watch, her dark face pale from the cold, she saw Marcel standing on the rocky knoll beside the house and pointing shoreward.

She ran up beside him and looked. There, in the

deep water between the island and the point, lay the supply-boat, rocking quietly on the waves.

It flashed upon her in a moment what it meant— the end of her fight, relief for the village, victory! And the light that had guided the little ship safe through the stormy night into the harbour was hers.

She turned and looked up at the lamp, still burning.

"I kept you!" she cried.

Then she turned to Marcel; the colour rose quickly in her cheeks, the light sparkled in her eyes; she smiled, and held out both her hands, whispering, "Now you shall keep me!"

There was a fine wedding on the last day of April, and from that time the island took its new name,— the Isle of the Wise Virgin.

THE END